T0063473

# Highlander

Joanne Stroud Hamilton

iUniverse LLC
Bloomington

# O HIGHLANDER

Copyright © 2014 Joanne Stroud Hamilton.

All rights reserved. No part of this book may be used or reproduced by any means, graphic, electronic, or mechanical, including photocopying, recording, taping or by any information storage retrieval system without the written permission of the publisher except in the case of brief quotations embodied in critical articles and reviews.

This is a work of fiction. All of the characters, names, incidents, organizations, and dialogue in this novel are either the products of the author's imagination or are used fictitiously.

iUniverse books may be ordered through booksellers or by contacting:

iUniverse LLC
1663 Liberty Drive
Bloomington, IN 47403
www.iuniverse.com
1-800-Authors (1-800-288-4677)

Because of the dynamic nature of the Internet, any web addresses or links contained in this book may have changed since publication and may no longer be valid. The views expressed in this work are solely those of the author and do not necessarily reflect the views of the publisher, and the publisher hereby disclaims any responsibility for them.

Any people depicted in stock imagery provided by Thinkstock are models, and such images are being used for illustrative purposes only.
Certain stock imagery © Thinkstock.

ISBN: 978-1-4917-2594-8 (sc)
ISBN: 978-1-4917-2593-1 (e)

Library of Congress Control Number: 2014903708

Printed in the United States of America.

iUniverse rev. date: 04/09/2014

AN


ODE TO THE PEOPLE OF THE HIGHLANDS


OF NORTH CAROLINA AND TO THE


DESCENDANTS


OF SCOTTISH HIGHLANDERS WHEREVER


THEY MAY LIVE.

Special Thanks to the Grandfather Mountain Highland Games and Gathering of the Clans for keeping the traditions going, and to the people of the Scotch Block at Milton, Ontario, Canada for my upbringing and values in the Scottish traditions.

In memory of Pipe Major Finn McCollum, our neighbor and hero to all the children of the area.

The characters in this book are fictional and the events are the flotsam and jetsam of a long life and the imagination of the author.

# Chapter 1

"MACKENZIE, Angus Alistair, 81, died Thursday, April 2nd, after a short stay in hospital. Pre-deceased by his wife, Janet, in 1998. Survived by his son, Brian, of the home. Cremation has taken place. A memorial service will take place at one p.m. on Saturday at St. Andrew's Presbyterian Church, Aberfoyle Springs."

So, old Angus had died. He suffered terribly from arthritis and asthma. He told my Grand-Dad that he wished he had gone when Janet passed.

"I'll go to this memorial, "I thought, as I folded away the newspaper, "Just to see Brian one more time."

My old church was sparsely attended for the memorial. I slid into the back pew behind a large woman with a big hat. We sang a few hymns and read together the 23rd Psalm, then, Reverend Alex Campbell spoke about Angus and how he liked to keep the Gaelic tongue, especially when reading the Bible. Alex read the 23rd Psalm again, but this time in Gaelic. Brian gave a short eulogy saying how his dad's suffering was finally at an end. Alex commended Angus' soul to the Lord.

Brian looked the same. So tall. So big. To my eyes, so handsome. Brian is the biggest man I have ever seen. Over six foot, eight with a big, wide body—but not heavy—lean and muscled. He didn't have to work out, because he worked hard.

He worked for the Roads Department of the County, and also worked the 200 acre farm, as well as caring for his aged parents. His hair was short, black and very curly. He was always quiet and kind of shy, although we could get him laughing.

Alex invited everyone to a reception in the church hall, prepared by the ladies of the church "and they assure me there are no calories, so enjoy," and he laughed, and then, said "Grace".

I went to the hall. The sweets looked delicious. The church ladies had quite a reputation for being good cooks. I ate a plain shortbread with an imprint of a thistle on it, product, I knew, of Mamie MacDougall, and had a cup of good strong tea. You hardly ever get strong tea anymore. I spoke to several people who recognized my funny-colored fair hair.

As I reached for the doorknob to leave, the door opened. It was Brian. We stared at each other.

"Georgia."

"Brian."

"Can I take you for a coffee?"

"I just had a tea," I stepped out and he shut the door behind me.

"I'm just going in to thank the ladies. They won't expect me to stay. I have a reputation of being anti-social to maintain. Can we talk somewhere?"

"I'll meet you at the Conservation Park."

"I won't be long."

"I'll wait."

I parked and walked over to see the ducks and swans. It wasn't long before an old green pickup truck parked and he got out. I walked further around the lake to a more secluded bench. He came along and sat beside me.

"You're all grown up, Georgia. I never thought you'd be this tall."

"Five foot ten and a half."

"But you are so slim."

"One fifteen to one twenty, but I'm all muscle."

"Are you too sophisticated to feed the ducks?" He took a large dinner roll out of his pocket. "You always fed the wild birds and kept the feeders full. I couldn't believe my eyes the first time I saw you feeding a chickadee out of your hand."

"We always liked seeing you when you came to turn around in our barnyard with either the grader or the snowplow."

"You kids were the best. I felt you were the younger sister and brothers I never had. Your dad was so interesting. He noticed little things that ordinary people never noticed."

"He taught us to see rainbows in mud puddles even when they were only caused by oil slick on the road."

"Is the family well?"

"You knew Grand-Dad died. Your dad sent a card."

"Does your dad still have that good job?"

"Oh, yes. He's Operational Manager now. It was lucky that job came up when it did. After his bowel resection, he could never work manually again, but there was nothing wrong with his brain."

"I missed you bunch so much. The corporation that bought your farm have never fit into the community and now the farm has become an exclusive golf club. Are you married?"

"Heavens, no! I've been going to college and working hard. You aren't either, are you?"

"No. I never saw a woman that came up to my ideal vision. The women around here want to go partying, drinking and bed-hopping when they're not shopping and going to the spa. The guys at work are hard-pressed to say they even like their wives. They don't even get a home-cooked meal out of it."

"You don't look like you do either."

"Not since Mom died. Dad and I never knew how spoiled we were. Neither of us could cook a thing, so the meals have been miserable. We went out to a restaurant for a meal once in a while then, wondered why we spent good money on bad food."

"I thought in church you looked very down in the dumps. It can't be because your father died. You wouldn't want him to suffer a minute longer than he had to."

"You're right. I'm glad his pain is over."

"What is it, Brian?"

"I'm thinking of selling the farm."

"What! No! You can't."

"Well, what's the point? My dad and grandfather would be upset, but I can't keep on mindlessly doing what I've been doing for years—working full time at a tiring job and working full time on the farm. I've had to let a lot of things go by the wayside. There just aren't enough hours in the day. The income from the milk is what I work the farm for, but I could sell off the cows—they're purebreds."

"Brian, the milk income is important. If you ever let that go, you could never afford to get back into the milk business again."

"I know."

We were silent for quite some time.

"Do you remember when I got stuck up the hay mow ladder?" I asked as I threw out the last of the bun to the fowl.

"Sure do. Where were your parents that day?"

"They went to a cattle auction with Grand-Dad. Gran was making supper and keeping an eye on us. My brothers had climbed to the top of the barn and were running along the beams then jumping into the remaining hay in the mow. I thought it looked like fun, so I climbed to the top of the ladder, but no way could I run along the beams with nothing to hold onto, then I turned to climb back down and I just froze. I was too scared to move, never mind climb down. The boys got Gran and she tried to talk me down and when that failed, she told me to hold on tight until Dad got home, in an hour or so. After ten minutes, we heard the grader coming up the lane. My brothers ran out and flagged you down and the next thing I knew, you strolled in and said . . . ."

"Whatcha doing Georgia, and you replied 'Not much'. Then I climbed up and brought you down."

"It was more than that. You came up the ladder and wrapped your arm around my waist. It felt like a tree limb. You told me to turn and put both my arms around your neck. I did and you said I could close my eyes if I wanted. I closed my eyes and buried my face in your neck. I could feel how strong you were as we descended. Then I was down."

"You were so cute, Georgia. Your little face so flushed, freckled and sweet. Your eyes are green with brown and gold flecks—just like a trout stream. What color is your hair? It's like your mother's, but much more curlier."

"It's not blonde or red—it's called strawberry blonde."

"It's very pretty, especially long like you have it now."

"Thank you, Brian. It's easier to care for when it's long. When it's short it has no body and flies all over."

He smiled kindly at me.

"The second time you came to my rescue was when I was fourteen. The chain came off my bike and I had pushed it for over a mile. I was just approaching your driveway, when I heard the grader coming. You came over the hill from our place and you saw the problem right away."

"I jumped down and brought a screw-driver, put the chain back on and tightened it so it wouldn't come off again. You thanked me so politely. You were so lovely."

"When I got back on my bike and rode off, you watched me to make sure the bike worked, until I went over the hill."

"Actually, I was watching you and thinking why can't I find someone like that? So mentally, I put that picture of you on the bulletin board of my mind as my ideal woman. I've been looking for an older someone just like you ever since, and never have I seen anyone who even came close."

"When I went over the hill, I waved to let you know the bike was fine and I said a little prayer. I said 'Dear Lord, keep Brian safe and don't let him get married until I'm old enough to marry him'."

We looked into each other's eyes. A red flush moved up his tanned cheeks. "You're kidding! Georgia, I'm too old for you."

"No, you aren't. When I was ten, you were eighteen. When I was fourteen, you were twenty-two. The paper said your dad was eighty-one. You told us your dad was fifty when you were born, so that makes you thirty-one. I'm twenty-three."

"Wow! Your college education is sure paying off."

We laughed and laughed. Suddenly, the years fell away and we were as comfortable as we'd always been, joking, teasing and laughing. "Georgia, would you like to come to the farm? I have to milk the lassies soon and I could give you some supper."

"I'd love to. I've never been on your farm, but isn't the community as gossipy as ever?"

"Are you kidding? If gossip was an Olympic sport, they'd all have gold medals. Who cares? Once we go in the driveway, it's a different world."

# Chapter 2

This part of North Carolina was settled by Scottish Highlanders after the first sheep Clearances in Scotland, when wool was more valuable that human beings, so the tenant farmers were put off the land so sheep could graze unimpeded. One settler went back and advised how to emigrate free to this area. At first, the Scottish came to the coast, then, some moved inland. Others followed the rivers and reached the mountains. While the Scottish mistrusted the English, free passage, free tracts of land and no taxes for a few years had a giant pull for a people who had always been tenants. In Scotland, every inch of land, every fish, bird, animal or bit of vegetation belonged to the gentry. If you were sick or injured, you were thrown out and an able-bodied man took your place. If you were old or infirm, your family better be able to look after you, because you would be "turfed out". They came to North America in droves with their Scottish Presbyterian religion, honesty and integrity, finding that working for one's self was much more gratifying than generating profit for someone else.

The Second Clearance in 1842 was even crueler, with as many as two thousand families a day burnt out, put out on the road and herded to the west coast where they could learn to farm the rocks or get on a boat to North America. This wave to North Carolina moved to the mountains and terrain with which they were more familiar.

The wilderness they recognized, but the climate was something absolutely new to them. Mild winters, hot summers, cool evenings, and plantings that almost sprung up overnight—corn higher than a man's head; beans that clambered up seven foot poles and bore and bore; fruit only seen at home on the plates of the "muckety-mucks". Trout streams where anyone with a fishing line could fish without running the hazard of being shot as a poacher by a games-keeper and your wife and bairns turned out on the road the next morning.

It was the Promised Land and for a while mostly Scottish farmed here but prosperity brought more settlers. The Scots welcomed these neighbors who like themselves hated the Sassenachs (English), and there was safety in numbers. Gradually their Gaelic language was the dialect of the home and kirk (church), and American English was the coin of everyday trade. Many, right up to modern times, spoke Gaelic at home and sometimes at church, and could go back and forth in the two. The men still wore their kilts on special occasions such as weddings, Hogmannay (New Years), funerals and ceilidhs (dance parties sometimes also with story-tellers). There are more descendants of Scottish Highlanders in North Carolina than any other state, or country in the world, including Scotland.

When we arrived here, Irish-Americans, we were welcomed. Everyone knew no one suffered more than the Irish under the yoke of the English. The Scottish-Americans had been here for over a hundred years but they were still clannish, stubborn and very prideful. Kick one Scot and they all say "ouch" was a popular saying among the non-Scottish. They were excellent neighbors, keeping to themselves, but first on the scene when help was needed, even opening their wallets if required. Their social events were ceilidhs and were held in the community centers and everyone no matter your heritage, enjoyed reels, Gay Gordons, schottisches, waltzes, and a sort of polka. We were all Scottish on these occasions. The young loved these dances as they danced every dance, learning the steps from their elders.

Every year, folk flock to Grandfather Mountain for the Highland Games and the Gathering of the Clans, which is immensely enjoyed by all and sundry, whether Scottish or not.

# Chapter 3

I followed him as he turned in his driveway. It seemed strange not to continue to the dead end and our driveway. His drive went through a big woods, then suddenly, you were out in the sun and the fields that were ringed with woods on all sides, and the mountains rose on the north side, going almost straight up. It was a beautiful farm, a flat saucer of arable land between the mountains and the rolling foothills to the south. The drive came up to the house. He drove on and put the truck away in a huge drive shed. The house was a bungalow, all on one floor, made of grey limestone with a grey metal roof. The door frame and the woodwork shone snow white.

I waited until Brian came up to me and then we went into an entry with one window, a bench and a coat rack on the wall. He opened the inside door and I went into the kitchen, took four steps and stopped dead.

"I know, I know, it's old-fashioned," he said. "The floor could be cushion-floored or laminated." It was smooth fitted limestone tiles. "The cupboards could be ripped out and modern ones installed." The cupboards were bird's eye maple with dark cherry wood trim outlining each door and drawer, and each had a white porcelain knob with pale blue flowers on it. "The sink is ancient." It was a porcelain double sink with a draining board of the same material in the middle. The sinks were deep. Above the sink was a bank of four windows that were also over a portion of the counter-tops on each side. "Of course, the stove would have to go." It was the biggest wood stove I had ever seen, with two large warming ovens on top with white porcelain panels with a motif of pale blue flowers. On the left side, over the stove, was a wrought iron trivet that could swing out and hold a teapot. A water reservoir was on the right side. The large oven had a white porcelain face with pale blue flowers and a bigger than usual temperature gauge. The warming ovens and the oven had metal handles with porcelains grips that had tiny pale blue flowers. A door led out of the kitchen on the right of the stove, and another door was positioned on the next wall. "That old bake cupboard belonged to my grandmother. I could probably get a pretty penny for it. It's in excellent condition." It was a Hoosier hutch and cabinet. Behind the long, top door would be a large flour bin and sifter. Behind the roll-top would be a spice rack and ribbed glass canisters for things like tea and rice. The top of the cabinet was enamel and could be pulled out to make a big surface for rolling out pastry or kneading bread. The very bottom drawer of the cabinet would be a zinc-lined with a slide-across lid. It would be the bread box. The large big-door compartment would house bowls, measuring cups, and such. I knew because we still used my grandmother's Hoosier. Next came what looked like a church pew, painted periwinkle blue, behind an oak table with three pressed-back oak chairs drawn up around it. The pew and the chairs all had comfy, chintz cushions. Then there was a large refrigerator. "I'll have to clear everything out and modernize before I could put it up for sale. What do you think, Georgia?"

"If you touch one thing in this kitchen, I'll have to kill you."

"What?"

"It's the most beautiful, sweetest, homiest kitchen I have ever seen in my life."

He laughed. "Come, I'll show you the rest of the house, I have to get out of this suit and go milk the cows. Then I'll make us some supper."

There was an arch on the wall beyond the fridge that led to the living room, but on the east wall of the kitchen was a large window, then a blank space until you came to the fourth press-back chair in the corner. From the window to the entry porch door, there was nothing.

Going through the arch, there were double French doors on the far wall, leading out to a screened porch that would be cool in summer as it was on the north side facing the mountainside. An ornate carved spinet stood out from the doors.

On the left side of the room was a huge stone fireplace with a recliner chair on the left and a soft armchair on the right. A television set on a high stand stood behind the armchair. Facing the fireplace was a two-seater, chintz loveseat.

On the right wall, there was a five foot oak desk with a filing cabinet under one side and a bank of drawers under the other. A golden oak swivel chair was pulled up between the two. A wide window with frilly Priscilla curtains was next, then a large, bow-fronted curved glass, china cabinet with lots of crystal glassware and "Blue Willow" china.

The floor was highly polished maple. The walls were papered in a white satiny paper with moiré swirls—a lovely "Laura Ashley" kind of room.

A wide hall led down a passage and ended at a large window. The first door on the right led to Brian's room and I don't think the décor had been changed since he was in short pants. The second door led to a much larger room with two windows looking out towards the mountains. A huge carved four poster bed dominated the room which also held two sizes of dressers, a vanity dressing table and an upholstered bench. "The bed, dressers, vanity table and mirror, stool and the spinet all came from Scotland with my grandparents."

Across the hall from the master bedroom was a large bathroom with a huge white, clawfoot slipper bath tub with a circular shower ring mounted on the ceiling, a white toilet and sink and a large white armoire which I presumed was a linen closet. A big window looked out on the drive.

The first room on the left was a big pantry/laundry room with one small window, lots of wooden shelves and a medium-sized freezer. A door on the left led to the kitchen beside the stove. I went back into the kitchen and started the woodstove.

Brian came in wearing jeans and a red plaid shirt.

"Do you mind if I rummage around in your fridge and make supper? How long will you be?"

"Georgia, I didn't invite you here to make you cook."

"You already told me you are a lousy cook, so I better make the meal."

He laughed. "Well, that worked. I'll be about an hour." I admired his physique as he strode up the drive towards the barn. He was so tall, so muscular.

# Chapter 4

I checked out the fridge. There was more than half a pound of bacon, eggs, a pound of ground beef, a bowl of left-over potatoes with the mark of a spatula on one side, a bag of apples in the crisper and in a stoneware crock marked "Onions" on the counter top, held a bag of onions.

I checked the drawers to find where everything was— utensils, silverware, etc., and found a drawer of aprons. They were exquisite with embroidery, appliqué, and colorful bric-a-brac. Each one was a masterpiece. I chose the least ornate one—a mauve chintz with mauve trim around the bib and pocket.

I fed the stove and checked the oven temperature; chopped an onion; browned the ground beef and onion; greased a casserole dish and a smallish round pan; and mixed three quarters of the mashed potatoes with a beaten egg and a little milk. The oven was now up to three hundred and fifty degrees. I cored four apples and put them in the round pan with a little water. To the meat and onion, I added salt, pepper, flour and a little dry mustard, mixed it up and put it in the casserole dish; the doctored mashed potatoes went on top with a few scrapings of butter. This was Cottage Pie and in the oven it went. Brown sugar, a touch of flour, a butter knob, cinnamon, nutmeg and cloves stuffed the apples and into the oven they went.

In the freezer, I found a part bag of frozen peas which I poured into a pan with cold water and put it on the side of the stove lids. I had saved a tablespoon or two of the chopped onion and added that to the peas.

I went outside and had a look at the fenced garden which I had caught a glimpse of when Brian was putting the truck away. I walked around and there was what I was looking for—mint. I broke a sprig off to go in the peas and also picked a couple of azalea blossoms.

Back in the kitchen, I whipped up a pan of biscuits and put the kettle on the main lid, and warmed the teapot. In the china cabinet, I had spied an iridescent swan with an open back. The azaleas looked lovely in water in the swan as a centerpiece. The table was set, along with cloth napkins, ketchup, butter, salt and pepper, a jug of milk and a sugar bowl. On the counter, I set out a small jug in case there was any cream to go over the apples.

It was almost time and everything was done, so the casserole went into the warming oven, along with our plates. The biscuits went into the oven and I fed the stove to up the temperature. Three apples went into a soup bowl, while the last one went into a cereal bowl. The spiced toffee in the pan was equally poured over the apples, and the bowls went in the warming oven. I dumped the hot tea pot, added three tea bags and wet the tea. Brian went by the window as I filled the pot.

He brought in a small pail. "Jersey milk?" I asked.

"Yes. We followed your family's example. Until you people came, all the farmers shipped every ounce of milk and cream, and used Carnation canned milk for their own use. Your parents showed us that we should be using the real thing for our families. We bought a Jersey, like you had, and her milk is for the house. Nowadays, most of Elsie's milk goes in the bulk cooler, but I do keep a bit out for cereal and tea."

I poured some into the little jug and put it on the table.

"What smells so wonderful? Meat, spices, apple."

"Are you ready to eat?"

"Aye, I washed in the dairy when I was washing the milking machine parts."

I brought the casserole to the table and placed it on a wooden trivet. Peas were drained and put out in a fancy little flowered dish with a dab of butter and a sprinkle of salt. Biscuits went into a wicker basket with a cloth to cover them. I put out the teapot on a padded stand. Lastly I brought over the hot plates.

"How did you do all this in one hour?"

"You better taste it first. If you fall off your perch, you may not be so enthusiastic. Will you take my hands?' He stretched out his hands and mine disappeared in them.

"I'll ask the blessing. 'Heavenly Father, be with us and lead us, and bless this food to our use and us to Thy service, and fill our hearts with grateful praise.' Amen."

I withdrew my hands and ladled out the Cottage Pie for both of us—one scoop for me and three for Brian; then I passed the peas to him. He took a small amount and passed them back. I took a small amount and passed them back. "Please take all the peas. They don't make good leftovers. They go all wrinkly."

As I poured the tea, he said, "Georgia, this is delicious. The best meal made in this house since Mom passed."

As he started clearing his plate with the last biscuit, I brought out the baked apple. "Georgia, you only have one apple. I don't need three."

"I can't eat two. I don't eat much. I love to cook and bake, but I've never been a big eater like my brothers. Eat what you want and you can have the rest for your supper to-morrow night."

"I remember you won first prize for your chocolate cake at the Fair."

"Yes, I did. I entered the Women's Division for the first time."

"After you left, the women went after the judge. They told him you were only thirteen and you should have been in the kid's division. The judge with the wisdom of Solomon told them,' Ladies, we didn't ask any of you your age so I had no way of knowing the age of the baker. It was the best chocolate cake I ever tasted. If I were you, I'd ask her for the recipe or she'll beat you every year'."

"Oh, I never knew they complained. I'd been baking since I was six."

We cleared the table and wrapped the rest of the food in film, so he could finish it the next day, and then we did the dishes.

"I'd better call my parents and let them know I'm going to be late."

"I wish you could stay longer. I hate to see you go. Georgia, I've laughed more to-day than I have in years."

"Well, I could call home and then I could call the Fairfax Motel and get a room. Thank goodness, I always have my toothbrush with me."

I called my family and Dad answered. I told him I was at Brian's and I would get a room at the Fairfax and be home to-morrow.

"Okay, honey. How is he? Is he down in the dumps?"

"Yes."

"Well you cheer him up and we'll see you to-morrow. If you go to church say hello to Alex and tell Brian I said hey."

"Dad says hey. Can I see your phone book?"

He went rummaging through drawers further along, while I hung up the linen tea towels and the dish cloth on the dowelled dryer by the stove.

Just as he handed it to me, the phone rang. He answered and signed off after just a few minutes with "Don't worry, Jim. She'll be fine."

"That was my Dad."

"Your mother and father talked it over and came to the same conclusion as I had. The Fairfax is next door to the Fox's Den, a really tough biker bar. Your Dad said if someone saw you going into a motel room alone, that door would be kicked in, in no time flat. I was thinking the same thing but I couldn't come up with an alternative. Your dad asked me if I could put you up for the night. He told me he trusts me to keep you safe. He's right. You'll be fine here. Shall we sit in the living room? The fire is laid. I'll just put a match to it."

I sat on the loveseat and he came and sat beside me. The sun was just setting and the fire was starting. We didn't put any lights on.

"Georgia, you wanted to marry me at fourteen. How do you feel about it at twenty-three? Will you marry me . . . . ?

# Chapter 5

"You betcha! Do you know I kept up a subscription to the Clarion, and every week I tortured myself, afraid I would read your wedding or engagement announcement, and each week, I breathed a sigh of relief until the next edition arrived."

"Oh, Georgia. I tried to put you out of my mind. I knew how smart you are, so I thought you would go to university or college and meet someone of your age and caliber and make an excellent match."

"There was never anyone else for me but you, and I had come to the conclusion it would never happen and I had to get on with the rest of my life. I finished college two weeks ago and have applied to five different jobs, only one of which is in North Carolina, two up north, one in Georgia, and one in Tennessee. I saw your dad's death notice in the paper and I came just to see you one last time and then go away, never to see you again."

"Georgia, why didn't you come looking for me? You must have known I was right here."

"I had learned to live with unrequited love, but if I got here and you were living with someone and had a string of kids, or if you wondered what on earth I could possibly want by coming here and told me so, I would have been so shattered."

We sat for a few minutes. "Did you ever think of looking me up?"

"No. I figured you had grown up and moved on and what would your family have thought—what an old fool! They might have laughed and said you married long ago."

"They would never think anything negative about you, anyway, they knew I had never gotten over you."

"Lucky I opened that door when I did, and there you were, like a dream. Ten minutes later and we would have been gone our separate ways forever."

He slid his arm across the back of the loveseat and took my hand with his other hand. "I decided I would never marry since I'd never even had a girlfriend, and what was the purpose of killing myself further with two jobs. No one to share the farm with and no one to leave it to, so I might as well sell up and become a drifter and see some of this country before the money ran out." I snuggled up to him and rested my head against his neck.

"All these years, I've been looking for someone just like Georgia McGee, when actually, I was looking for Georgia McGee. Are you sure you want to marry me?"

"Aye." He held me tight.

"Would you expect me to get a job?"

"I suppose you want to put all this education you got into use. I can understand that, so, if that's what you want to do."

"It's not what I want to do at all. I want to look after you and help you with the farm so you don't have to work so hard. You know I never wanted to leave our farm, but after Dad had his Crohn's Disease bowel resection, there was no way he could ever do physical work again. In high school, I worked a twelve hour shift every Saturday, year round, at a nursery that also had greenhouses, and still managed to get honors every year. The last year, I won a big scholarship which ensured I could go to any university or college I wanted. I used it to go to agricultural college. The first year, I took "Field Crops" which represented every crop ever heard of, plus new crops. We found out all soybeans and corn are genetically modified, meaning growth hormones to increase the harvest, but not improve it. We studied a grain called quinoa, which you will be hearing lots about. Have you seen the Chinese wearing masks because the pollution is so bad? Well, the water is polluted from the air and rice grows in water. The rice for Chinese consumption is grown far from the cities. The polluted rice is exported to America for us to enjoy.

Each year, as soon as college ended in May, I was on a train two days later to Minnesota or Wisconsin to plant trees for the government reforestation program.

The nursery had no problem hiring two males for my job for the summer at student rate. I won another scholarship, which paid for my second year—"Animal Husbandry". My parents insisted on paying for my dorm room, as they wanted me on campus for the access to the library, computer labs, cafeteria, and for safety. I paid for my books, trying to get used, but buying new, if I had to. "Animal Husbandry" means I can clear a blocked teat on a cow, emasculate young pigs, and all phases of breeding and raising of animals. I won another scholarship, which kept me in college, taking "Organic Farming and Gardening for Health and Profit". Another scholarship and I took "Forestry" for my final year, which means I have a paper that says I can timber cruise your woods, inventory the trees, show what looks healthy but may be a host for disease My aim was always to return to a farm somewhere and use my knowledge. I applied to be a Farm Manager."

"We are going to have fun farming, aren't we?"

"I hope so. By the way, I know how to run milking machines. Can we walk the farm to-morrow?"

"Sure. From now on, I'll be the brawn if you'll be the brains."

"Do you go to church?"

"I haven't for quite some time. Dad couldn't endure the wooden pews, even with a cushion, and I didn't like to leave him alone. He was alone all week in the daytime. Besides, I was sick of everyone pushing their unwed relatives at me. Dad and I paid our tithe and Alex came and gave us communion. Alex understood the shifting spinster attendance and commiserated with me. After we get married, I would be very proud to go every Sunday with you. When would you like to get married?"

"Perhaps we need time to get to know each other as two adults? Maybe I'm a scold or a nag or a sniffer."

"Sniffer? What's that?"

"After every statement make a nasty sniff sound. You know," and I gave him a demonstration.

"Ruby Montgomery."

"Oh, my, yes. I wasn't thinking of anyone in particular, but how does Everett put up with that noise?"

"I think we'll get used to each other pretty quickly. I was at your house all the time until you moved away. Your Dad and I studied farm papers, talked about politics, and he told me about philosophy and literature. I never had a library card until I got to know him."

We had a cup of tea before retiring. The fire burned low, so Brian had put on the furnace. The furnace was natural gas and the deal was if they transverse your land with the gas line, you can have gas piped in, payment for the access. You still pay for gas usage. The furnace was located outside and could be switched to air conditioning by the control in the house.

Brian told me there were clean sheets on the huge bed in the big bedroom. He put out a set of mauve towels for me, then, opened the top drawer of the smaller dresser. "Dad and I never had the guts to get rid of Mom's clothes. Leila O'Halloran comes once a month to wash and clean. She was here on Friday and changed the bed linen. Once a year, she launders Mom's things and puts them back. This top drawer contains nightgowns and underwear. Just help yourself, and after you come here, I'd appreciate if you did something with them—give them to some charity or other." I kissed him good-night. "See you are exactly the right height," he murmured. He left. I went to bed with my head in a whirl.

# Chapter 6

In the morning, I was awake at four-thirty, went into the bathroom, then back to the bedroom. I checked in the wardrobe and took out a fleecy robe, nipped into the kitchen and started the woodstove. Back in the bedroom, I came to the conclusion that Mrs. MacKenzie must have been my size as a pair of underwear and a pair of soft blue slacks fit perfectly. I donned a flowered shirt over my bra. I hoped Brian wouldn't be dismayed to see me wearing his mother's clothes. I could always put my suit back on, although it wasn't too practical for looking at outbuildings.

I heard Brian go into the bathroom and I went back into the kitchen and put the kettle on. He had time for breakfast before chores, and I hoped he liked to eat first, not after. I started frying bacon. The joys of the warming oven is, it keeps food hot but doesn't cook it any more. I peeled an onion and chopped a small section, wrapping the remainder and putting it in the fridge. The onion bits were mixed into the remaining mashed potatoes, and then went into a small frying pan with melted butter.

"Good morning, sweetheart."

Oh, he looked so handsome. I put my arms around his neck. He was tender, warm and yet so strong.

"How do you like your eggs?"

He laughed. "Anyway you want to fix them, love."

"Well, I imagine you mostly fry, so how about poached eggs on toast?"

"Wouldn't that be a nice change?" He went and sat down. I poured him out a tea to get started, and set the table.

"I didn't know if you preferred coffee?"

"Nope, raised on tea. I get coffee at lunchtime, but we don't even own a coffee pot. We could get one of those drip ones, if you like."

"We never had the teapot empty for long, either."

I poured hot water out of the kettle into the small round pan and added some vinegar. It started rippling immediately, so I pushed it to one side to keep it simmering but not boiling. The eggs were broken, one at a time, onto a saucer and slipped into the pan. Suddenly, we were side by side. "I never knew how to poach an egg. It's a shame, too, because it was my Dad's favorite way to eat eggs." I punched down the bread in the toaster.

He sat back down. "You look lovely in that shirt and slacks."

"Are you sure you don't mind? I can put my suit back on."

"No. If you can use the clothes, help yourself. Wouldn't my mother like to know my wife liked her choice in clothes?"

"I don't have a lot of clothes, mostly work clothes or tees and jeans for school." I put his plate before him.

"Wow. I could get used to this."

"I hope you will," and I poured out tea.

It was a beautiful morning. After he went to the barn, I did the dishes, swept the floor, and made my bed. I looked in Brian's room, but his bed was made.

I helped myself to a pair of rubber boots and a light jacket and headed to the barn. Next to the house, in full southern sun was the vegetable patch. Looking over the gate at the overgrown weeds and rampant vegetables, I could see a line of raspberry bushes on the right hand side, badly in need of a pruning and weeding. On the left fence, asparagus, needing to be picked, growing up through its debris of former years. Between the two fences, you could make out the outlines of raised beds. The garden measured twenty-five feet by fifty feet. Beyond was the chicken house, now silent and empty, with the run on the side and behind. I mentally measured running feet for fencing. The pig sty was next, fenced and tidy, but no piggies. The huge drive shed was next with his truck, big tractor, hay wagon, lots of implements and a tool shed.

When I entered the barn, the lassies all turned to look at me with great curiosity. Brian made the introductions. They were lovely Guernsey cows plus a petite, doe-like Jersey. I would remember to bring apple slices next time.

The barn was clean and tidy with fresh straw in every stall. A tabby cat brushed against my legs. "Hello". I gave his ears a scratch. "What's his name?"

"Barney and he's the best mouser you ever saw. There's no Mrs. Barney—he's fixed." Brian opened the door at the end of the barn and then the lassies trooped out. I watched them go. The gate to the pasture was open and they headed in different directions, munching as they went.

"You keep a clean barn, Brian," I said, admiring the white-washed walls and the spotless woodwork of the many shining glass windows, as he came back in from closing the pasture gate.

"Thank you. It's so much easier and cheaper to be clean than fight disease."

# Chapter 7

As we walked towards the house with his arm around my shoulder and the Jersey milk pail in the other hand, he said," I was thinking of buying a new pickup truck."

"To go drifting in?"

He laughed. "That was the plan, but still I think it's time for a new one."

"Will you trade in the old one?"

"It runs good and the tires are only a couple of years old, and it had a brake job last year. I always keep the maintenance up to date, but they probably won't offer me much for it."

"Why don't we trade in my old car instead and I could use the truck?"

"Wouldn't you mind?"

"How many bags of feed and how many rolls of fencing can you get in an old Mercury Topaz?"

He laughed. "What would you change first?"

"Do Scott's still sell pullets and piglets?"

"Sure."

"Well, first I'd whitewash the inside of the sty and the henhouse; repair any fencing; then put three pigs in the sty and six hens in the henhouse. Then, it's overdue, but the garden should be planted."

"I let those things go. I just didn't have the time. I'll warn you, though you probably remember, there's hawks, owls and vultures in those woods," and he waved his hand towards the mountainside.

"I remember."

We turned and looked over the fields, most of which were lying fallow—unplanted to a crop. A small grassy orchard was on the left side of the drive, across from the drive shed.

"Then I'd cruise the woods and inventory every tree. Rumor has it that the government could send in a timber cruiser to do the same thing and then they could come back in five years, cruise it again, and you will pay income tax on the value of the missing trees, whether you sold them or used them for firewood and fence posts."

"You're kidding."

"No, that's the latest we were told. Even now, if you sell to a lumber company, you have to declare it as income. If you make a contract with the government to replant every tree cut with a similar tree or one they approve, you can get a tax reduction and defer any tax."

When we came back to the kitchen, Brian put the kettle on.

"Can I show you something?" I asked, reaching for my purse. He came and squatted down beside my chair.

"I don't have much, but I'm not exactly empty handed." I handed him my bankbook.

"You've been in school. How could you accumulate over twenty thousand dollars? Every other student comes out of university or college owing thirty to fifty thousand in student loans."

"I told you I always worked. One twelve hour shift every Saturday all through high school and all winter long during college. I won scholarships that paid the tuition, plus I went tree planting four summers. I always tried to get used books for the next year's courses, but if I couldn't get used I'd buy new, and took them with me. While the other tree planters were out carousing and spending their money as fast as they earned it, I was pounding the books. By the time I came home, I had been through the books at least once and my money was intact. That's how I won scholarships every year. This is my savings account and I do have a small checking account."

"You are amazing. I'm glad I proposed before you showed me that or you would have thought I was after your money."

"Did you hear about the farmer that won the million dollar lottery and they asked him what he was going to do with the money? He thought a few minutes, then he said, 'I guess I'll just go on farming until I go broke'." We laughed because we knew farming could be a money pit.

He poured out the mugs of tea, while I put out sugar and milk. The spoons were on the table in a cut-glass holder on the table. He left the room by the hall door by the Hoosier and came right back.

"Here's my savings account and here's my Dad's. His is a joint account, so I have to close it and transfer the money into my account. The farm was transferred into my name when I turned eighteen, but they didn't tell me until I was twenty-one. Dad was afraid of inheritance tax like they have in Britain."

I was amazed at the figures in the books. "So we are financially fit going into this marriage, and it's up to us to keep it that way?"

"That's the picture, but somehow, I don't think you would spend foolishly. I think you are as careful with money as I am."

"Tighter than bark to a tree, is how my Dad describes me. My brothers like to spend and then want to borrow from me, but no way will I lend a dime. I do pay my church tithe and support a children's charity, but no one but you has any idea how much I have saved."

"Let's get serious. When do you want to get married?—this afternoon, to-morrow, Saturday or six months from now?"

"To-morrow would be nice, but, no, how about next Saturday?"

"How does one go about getting married in North Carolina?"

"Don't know. Look at the time. Let's go to church. It should be getting out in ten minutes. Alex can tell us and of course, it will depend on when he can do it."

I popped my suit back on and Brian changed into better clothes. We parked our vehicles across the street. As the last person left, we went in the door. "Alex", Brian called as we closed the big door behind us. He was half-way up the aisle, and turned back to us.

"Hello, Georgia. I heard you were at the memorial and I looked for you but you were gone. How is the family?"

"They are all fine, thank you. Alex, how can we get married?"

He looked awestruck. "Let's go to my office."

We sat down in the two chairs provided, facing him as he sat down on the desk and took our hands solemnly.

"If I'd thought about it for a lifetime I would never have thought I would hear that request from you two. Georgia, how old are you?"

"Twenty-three."

"And you, Brian."

"I just turned thirty-one."

He looked at us for a minute or two. "Let's pray." He prayed for guidance and then asked God to bless our decision. "When would you like to get married?"

"Saturday," we both said.

He got up and looked in his diary. "Two o'clock alright?" We agreed and then asked how we could get a license. He told us we had to go to the County Registrar's office. "Take all your credentials—driving licenses, birth certificates and social security numbers. It will cost you fifty dollars and I suggest you take cash as you would have to wait for a check to clear. There is no waiting period. You can get married five minutes after you get the license, and there is no blood test. Bring the license with you on Saturday, along with your witnesses. You'll sign papers, the witnesses will sign and I will sign and forward it to the Registrar."

"Thanks, Alex. We'll see you at two o'clock on Saturday."

"Georgia, Brian, you are two of my favorite people. I would never have put you two together, but I'm delighted you found each other. A word of advice. Don't try to outdo each other in work. I know you are both hard workers and always have been, but marriage is not a competition. You must pull together to make it work. My old grandmother in Scotland had a sure-fire way to make a couple do that. You still burn some wood, don't you, Brian? Well, take out the cross-cut saw, one on each end, and cut up your firewood. The saw only works if you work together. Bless you children. Brian, your dad would be so pleased. He was worried sick about what would happen to you after he was gone." Then he put his hands on our shoulders and said a short prayer in Gaelic.

In the stone archway, in front of the church, we parted with a kiss.

"Your family will be shocked."

"No, they won't. They have always known that I loved you. My mother keeps telling me to forget about you and get on with the rest of my life. I finally came to her conclusion. We've had a narrow escape. By year's end, you could have been adrift, while I could have been on my way to being a dried up old miseryguts of a spinster."

He laughed, "Well, we have saved the world from a pair of old miseryguts!"

"Do you still have a kilt?" Most of the old families kept the tradition of the men wearing their kilts at special times.

"Would you like me to wear it? I was thinking about it, but didn't know what you would think. I wouldn't want to outshine the bride."

"You can try."

"What time do you want to meet on Friday to get the license?"

"Is three alright with you?"

"Perfect, I'll see you there. Bring all your old divorce papers."

"Bring your parole officer!"

He lifted me up and spun around, both of us laughing like kids. Finally we parted. His last request was he wanted Gran for his witness.

# Chapter 8

On Friday, we jumped through the hoops and got the license. Mom had come with me and Brian hugged her. I gave him a new picnic basket with his supper inside and a grocery list. He opened a jeweler's box and showed us the two rings inside. Both were braided 24 carat gold bands. His was a huge circle, while mine was tiny. I tried it on. "Fits perfect but how did you know the size?"

"It was the smallest they had."

On Saturday, I followed Dad as we drove through a nasty rainstorm, but it let up the other side of Asheboro, and by the time we got near the mountains, it was a beautiful, sunny day. The spring had been unusually cold and extended, but finally the weather was warmer and the flowering trees were coming out. We had a light lunch at a roadside café, but I only nibbled, as I was too excited.

We got to the church first and went in. Alex warmly greeted my family as they were all old friends. Suddenly the big door swung open, and there he was in all his glory! Gone was the quiet, shy big man and in his place stood a mighty

Scottish warrior, the kind to strike terror into the heart of an opponent. His kilt was navy blue with faint yellow and red stripes. His coat was navy velvet with brass buttons; his white collarless shirt had a large frill of lace at his throat; his sporran (purse) that hung from chains at his waist was grey wolf fur; his high snow-white socks were topped with navy ribbons and tassels, and his shoes were brogues called "ghillies" that laced up. As he approached, I looked down at my pale blue velvet dress and mouthed at him "You win." He laughed. My Dad stepped up to grasp Brian's arm and shake his hand. Brian then hugged Mom as he had the day before, and then he stooped to hug and kiss Gran on the cheek.

Mrs. Haggard, the organist, waved to us, and as we started up the aisle and steps, she played "Here Comes the Bride". We made our vows and embraced. It was a very emotional moment for both of us as we gazed into each other's eyes.

As we signed the necessary papers, Mrs. Haggard softly played "Amazing Grace". Gran sat and signed. Mom and Dad signed next. I stepped over to Mrs. Haggard, gave her a hug and an envelope. Alex had advised that the going rate was twenty dollars to the organist and fifty dollars to the minister. Mrs. Haggard's envelope held fifty dollars and Alex's one hundred.

There were handshakes and hugs all round.

"Will you come to church to-morrow?" asked Alex.

"We'll be here," Brian confirmed.

"Please wear your kilt and Georgia, your lovely dress. I'd like to introduce you to the congregation and officially declare hunting season over," and he gave Brian a big wink.

As we walked to the door, Mrs. Haggard loudly played "Scots Wha Hae".

# Chapter 9

We went to the farm, while Dad dropped into the local deli and came away with a pre-ordered meal in several bags. We changed clothes, while Mom and Gran admired the kitchen. Brian gave the tour as we talked of our aspirations. At four-thirty, Mom and Gran shooed us into the living room while they set out a buffet on the counter tops. We loaded our plates with smoked salmon, salad vegetables, small toasts and crackers with pate, salsa, olives, pickles and cheese, potato salad and coleslaw. Dessert was squares, tarts and cookies we had made at home. Dad opened champagne and presented us with six champagne flutes.

"I didn't think you would have any flutes as I know your mother was strictly teetotal."

"You're right. The house was alcohol-free, but Dad kept a bottle of whiskey in the barn, and when haying in the summer, he and I would each have a beer. We chilled the bottles in the barn sink with ice cubes. After Mom died, Dad brought the bottle in. A tot at bedtime allowed him to rest easier."

Father proposed a toast as we sat down around the kitchen table. Brian and I sat side by side on the periwinkle pew.

When they left, we stood with an arm around each other and waved good-bye.

I packed away the leftovers while Brian went to the barn.

Later we sat on the loveseat in front of a small fire.

"I want to show you something." I turned on the lamp on the end table. After digging in my purse, I handed him a paper. It was the results of a physical examination I had two days before.

"'This is a medical report. Is it telling me something is wrong?"

"It's telling you I am in A-one condition."

"Why would I need to know that? You look healthy to me."

"Well, Doctor MacKenzie, I wanted to know before I married you if my health was one hundred percent. No way did I want to saddle you with a person with a serious illness or someone whose medication costs would bring you to your knees."

"What a funny girl you are."

"Do you see this line—intact? It means I'm a virgin."

"I didn't need proof."

"You know the young bucks in this county. They don't care they are shredding some poor girl's reputation while lying and bragging about their sexual conquests."

"You are right about that."

"I wouldn't want some smart aleck saying, 'Georgie McGee—I had her in the back seat of my father's Buick last summer'. You might not believe it but it could taint how you thought about me and I wouldn't even know. Here's proof."

"Okay, sweetheart, if you feel better being completely honest with me, I'm fine with that."

"Well, I wouldn't buy a horse without having a look at its teeth."

Brian started laughing. "I don't buy horses. I'm a dairyman, remember. Guess what I check."

I laughed. "I udderly understand."

We put the television on and caught the end of the Braves games, which we both enjoyed. Brian went to the kitchen and brought two glasses of soda. One sip made me say, "What is that?"

"It's rum and coke. I know you don't drink, and I don't usually, but I thought we might just enjoy a drink to relax us." We sipped our drinks.

"Are you as nervous as I am?"

"You're not the only virgin in the house."

"People have been cohabiting since the dawn of time and it must be enjoyable. When God said go forth and multiply, he must have made sex pleasurable or couples would only have one child and never attempt it again. I don't think the world would have become populated by just one child per couple."

"We will be fine, sweetheart. You'll see," and he lifted me up and carried me down the hall, snapping off lights as we went. I felt so safe and sheltered in those mighty arms.

# Chapter 10

In the morning, I was up first, showered and dressed in the clothes I had put out in the linen closet the night before. I got the woodstove going and made up pancake batter, browned sausages and put them in the oven to finish cooking and drain the fat off. I set the table and put maple syrup in a small pan off to the side of the burner lids to warm.

"Are we still in love?" He stood at the kitchen door by the Hoosier. His curly black hair was still damp from the shower.

"More than ever." We wrapped our arms around each other. "What are you making this morning?"

"Pancakes and sausages."

"Oh, wow. I'll be putting weight on."

"No, just a little bit, but then you'll taper off. I hope you like fruit and vegetables, fish and cheese, and I use olive oil instead of lard or butter for cooking."

"I love fruit and vegetables, but for one, it can get pretty monotonous if you have to munch your way through a bag of lettuce on your own."

"You'll see. You'll never munch alone again. It's called the Mediterranean Diet and it's very healthy, and it's not all twigs and berries. Do you have a fig tree?"

"No, do you want one?"

"Yes, please, in a sheltered spot. Figs are very good for you—with a dribble of honey, baked and served with Greek yoghurt, they are delicious."

Before we ate, Brian said, "I'll ask the blessing." We joined hands. "Thank you, Lord, for bringing us through the night with dignity, respect and love. Thank you for this day. This is the start of our journey together. Bless this food to our use and us to Thy service through our Savior, Jesus Christ. Amen."

We smiled at each other. His big brown eyes crinkled at the corners. He had square, white teeth; a hawk's sharp beak for a nose, and when he really smiled like he was doing now, dimples winked into view on each cheek.

After breakfast, I did the dishes, and tidied the bedroom. I walked out to meet him.

"So I can get some hens?"

"Sweetheart, you can have anything you want."

"Well, right now, anyway, in the first blush of marriage," I chuckled. He laughed.

"We'd better get ready for church soon."

I put the creamy milk away. Lunch would be salmon sandwiches with the leftover items. Roast beef with roasted potatoes, carrots and onions for supper.

On our arrival at church, I went in first and slid into the back pew. When church started and all eyes were on the front, Brian slipped in beside me.

Alex was in fine fettle this morning, rolling his rrrs like thunder. He was a powerful speaker. Presbytery kept trying to retire him, he kept resisting and his congregation was very adamant in their attempts to keep him. After the sermon, Alex drew everyone's attention to the sick and shut-in. Then he said, "I have the great privilege this morning to introduce this congregation to our newlyweds. Folks, let me present Mr. and Mrs. Brian MacKenzie. Mrs. MacKenzie is the former Miss Georgia McGee. I had the great honor of performing their wedding yesterday. Please show your pleasure."

We stood and there was loud applause. Alex then said a prayer for the ill and gave us a blessing. People were most kind, congratulating us and welcoming me back into the fold.

# Chapter 11

It was a beautiful day and Brian put a table under the kitchen window on a small paved patio, and brought two big wicker chairs from the drive shed. I prepared plates for us—large for Brian and small for me. I'd also made freshly-squeezed orange juice.

As we sat at our leisure, a couple of titmice came by with friendly comments. We threw some small pieces of crust for them, and they were immediately joined by a Carolina Wren, with way too much to say for himself. Soon a quiet little chickadee came to the party.

"What kind of rose is that by the door?"

"It's called 'Zepherine Drouin', it's French. The sweetest smelling rose. Soon the whole column will be covered with little roses. The climber at the other end of the window is called 'Galway Bay' and it's an Irish beauty. My mother could really raise roses. She did the garden as well. I'll cut down the garden and then I can work it for you."

"I can work the beds. I only need one bed to get the salad greens started, then I can work the others."

"It'll take you quite a while."

"No, it won't. The hens will become chicken tractors."

"Chicken tractors?" he squawked, imitating a chicken.

"I'll put a cage of fencing over the first four feet of a raised bed. Put a hen inside and a water bottle and away she'll go—scratching out bugs, weeds, seeds and cultivating and fertilizing as she goes. Six hens—six beds being worked. Move the cage forward four feet and they're back in business. The beds will be worked and ready for planting in three or four days."

He chuckled and shook his head. "This I gotta see."

After work on Monday, he arrived with a steel pole with arms. He pounded it into the ground just off the patio edge, but in front of the kitchen windows over the sink. He drove into the drive shed and returned with three different kinds of bird feeders—a steel niger seed holder, a suet cage and a big tubular feeder for mixed seed. I came out and examined them.

"Thank you, love, we can enjoy our little friends even more."

"What did you do with your day?"

"First, I called my insurance company and added you as an occasional driver. Then I went into town and bought some white wash lime, red barn paint and white exterior paint for trim. I got some of the first strawberries from Mrs. McCarty. She said the cold weather has made them late, but the berries are plentiful, huge and sweet. I white-washed the interior of the henhouse and the pig sty, using a roller. You know, Brian, in Britain and in Europe, pigs are raised free-range in a field with little metal Quonset huts that are open on both ends and have straw inside. Free range pork, as you can imagine, demands a higher price."

"What field would you put them in?"

"Just three pigs this year, so we'll have two to sell and one for us. Next year, the field on the left of the drive would be good. They could forage in the orchard and keep it clear of weeds, as long as we didn't use toxic spray on the fruit trees."

"I like the idea. Let's keep that in mind for next year. I'll phone my insurance company to-morrow and get you covered as spouse."

For supper, I had cut the asparagus spears that were ready, made pastry and what we always called 'egg and onion pie', but was now elegantly referred to as 'quiche'. We had it with the asparagus and a tossed salad with an orange vinaigrette dressing and those fresh strawberries with Jersey cream for dessert.

Then I did the dishes; he wanted to help but I made him sit and tell me about his day. Then I asked to see the basement which I hadn't seen to date. As the furnace was outside, the basement was cool and there was shelving lined with clean jars waiting to be filled. There was a huge work bench with a long fluorescent light over it. I studied the light.

"What are you thinking? I can hear the wheels turning."

"I think I just found my greenhouse."

"In a basement?"

"Sure. It's an even temperature, not too hot or too cold. The fluorescent light can have longer chains and can be lowered and raised and have a timer installed. A small flower grower was one of the places I visited during 'Organic Farming and Gardening for Health and Profit' She raised all her plants in the basement filled with long tables, moving the lights down low for the seeds to grow and raising them as the plants grew taller. At the right time, she moved her stock to her real greenhouse business."

"Don't you need special bulbs?"

"She used ordinary fluorescent, not the expensive grow lights."

"What would you start down here? Tomatoes and peppers?"

"Everything in peat pots, then right into the garden at the proper planting time. It only pays if you have a lot of plants going at once, otherwise the power company might think the power costs are suddenly too high and think you are raising marijuana."

"There's an idea. So many veterans and young people smoke 'weed', it could be a money-maker."

"Not until it's legal, Brian, if it ever will be."

"Is it reasonable with the few plants for the garden? We are only two people."

"Two people devouring vegetables, preserving them, canning them, freezing them, and don't you think people at work would pay for organic vegetables if the price was kept down, and how about the elderly in the community, and at church to whom we could give a small quantity. Think of old Mrs. McArthur who always had a beautiful vegetable patch and now lives in an apartment at Sunset Retirement Center. Give her a paper bag with a couple big tomatoes and a handful of Tiny Tim tomatoes and watch her smile. And don't forget cos lettuce for the chickens and carrots and mangels for the cows and pigs."

"What are mangels?"

"Mangel-wurzel is the proper name. We refer to it as a kind of turnip or rutabaga, but actually it's a member of the beet family, used in Europe originally for cattle food and used in the Amish community in this country. You have to chop them up. You can partially cook them if you want. Carrots are also used for the same purpose."

He wrapped his arms around me. "Go, girl. Let's do it. And I thought I knew all about farming. I'm going to enjoy learning new things,"

"Brian, I'm not trying to find new work for you. This is just something for me to putter at. The object here is to ease your load, while feeding you well. Same with the hens, pigs and the wild birds. I'll do the work. You enjoy."

"We'll see. If you come to enjoy doing something, perhaps, it's not work. I'd like to help you can and make pickles. Mom always shooed us out of the house. Would you like a dehydrator to dry fruit and vegetables?" We were now sitting in the living room. I wrinkled up my nose.

"No. It concentrates the sugar and I'm not crazy about tough, chewy things or slimy reconstituted things, when I can freeze and have that fresh-picked flavor, so, no thank you."

"Now that you mention it, the fruit does taste and feel like . . . . ."

"Jerky."

"Exactly."

I went over to the spinet, sat down, opened the cover.

"Do you still play? I remember you played the piano one year at the Christmas Concert at the school."

"I took lessons for years from old Miss McDonald, but I haven't played for a long time." I opened a song book. "Oh, it's all in Gaelic." I started playing the notes. "Oh—it's 'Flow Gently Sweet Afton'."

"Play," he said huskily. He came over to turn the pages.

Soon we were singing all the old Scottish songs. His voice was low, but smooth as a pebble. My voice is not soprano, so our voices blended well. We sang every song in that book.

"Do you still play the bagpipes?"

"What makes you think I do?"

"We loved to hear the pipes on a still Sunday evening. Your dad had a breathing problem so no way did he have the lungs for it."

"I haven't played in a long time."

# Chapter 12

The white wash had to set for a few days. On Saturday, I borrowed Brian's truck and went for fencing, bins and then I went to Scott's where I bought six Buff Orpington hens for the wooden crate I brought with me, and three Yorkshire piglets that I put in a burlap bag in the back with the crate.

Brian had been mending fences, but came to help me unload. I had two big metal bins for the feed. The hens seemed a tad miffed at being shut up in a crate, but soon fluffed out their feathers and started sedately examining their surroundings, where as the piggies squealed and ran joyously around their pens, so happy to be free and out in the sunshine after a life of confinement in a pig barn.

That evening, I told Brian there didn't seem to be a baseball game as they had all been afternoon games.

"Do you like country music? Old country music?"

"Sure, we were raised on it. Mom and Dad never missed the Grand Ole Opry on radio or television. It was great then."

"Wait till I show you what I have." He went down the hall to his old room and came back with a large cardboard box, and a boom box (radio, CD and tape player). "I went to an auction sale that advertised there were old CDs and tapes. I got all these oldies for twenty dollars and the player for five. Maybe they are in rough shape and no good, but let's see what's in here,"

We carefully lifted each one out. He confided he's only seen the top layer and hadn't gotten back to try them out. If they were in good shape, what a treasure trove— Hank Williams, Merle Haggard, Johnny Cash, Hank Locklin, Stonewall Jackson, George Jones, Dolly Parton, Jeannie Shepherd, Kitty Wells, Loretta Lynn, and Webb Pierce—all updated from old 78's. We started playing them. We sat on the loveseat, wrapped around each other, and enjoyed a wonderful evening of music we both loved. There would be more such times.

"Brian, can you dance?"

"Are you kidding? Of course not. I'd love to be able to dance because I love music. How about you?"

"I'd love to dance, but I don't know how."

"You know there's a dance studio in Fraserville. They teach kids, but they advertise they teach ballroom dancing to adults. Their clientele, I imagine, is mostly seniors, but we wouldn't mind, if they didn't."

"I'll give them a call on Monday."

# Chapter 13

We did sign up for dance lessons. At first, the lady instructor danced with Brian, while I danced with an elderly gentleman with clicking false teeth which seemed to keep the beat. All the rest of the students were senior citizens who could dance but came here to do so. Soon, Brian and I were dancing together. The lady instructor was amazed at how light Brian was on his feet. We tried all the dances but we loved to waltz the best. We practiced at home and thought we were getting the hang of it. It was great fun. We had bought dance tapes. We twirled around the living room and then two-stepped to the kitchen and back.

"Soon we could try line dancing and rock and roll."

"Sure we can. We're really getting good."

"You know there's a spring dance at the country club, not the one at our old farm. You don't have to be a member to attend. It was advertised in the newspaper."

We decided to go, but we would only dance with each other. What a disaster! As we stepped on the dance floor, the lights went out except for the odd spot and the light over the bar. We were swept apart immediately. These middle—aged women, "cougars" I believe they are called, aggressively were all over Brian, leading him away to the center of the room, meanwhile the middle aged to old men were all around me, making sure I wouldn't dance with Brian. I was pawed and pulled this way and that, as each grabbed me around the waist and tried to press themselves against me. The room was so dimly lit I couldn't see Brian, and I'd been turned around in circles so much, I couldn't get my bearings. Even though I resisted, one old goat clasped me tightly and ran his hand down my back and pinched my rear. "Brian", I screamed.

"Back off you people. You okay, sweetheart?" He cut through the crowd like a hot knife through butter. "We're outta here!" He grabbed my hand and we rushed out to the truck. He held me close. "It's okay, now, babe." He held me tight against him as I shook.

"What a nightmare! We were swarmed, Brian."

Brian's experience was just as bad as mine. He had women draping themselves on him and grinding their hips against him. As he pushed one away, he was grabbed by another. The last one actually ran her hand up the inside of his thigh.

"When you screamed, I shoved that woman off and she sat down hard on the floor. I couldn't get to you fast enough. What a bunch of degenerates. Let's go home and have a cup of your wonderful cocoa."

As we drove, I told him, "You know what the trouble is? We were both raised to respect everyone, especially our elders. We are so naïve and unprepared for that kind of behavior."

We decided to keep our dancing limited to the dance studio and home.

"You know what's startling. Those people are the cream of our society. I saw the mayor holding up the bar with some bleached blonde. I'm pretty sure I saw my dentist there, and the woman with the roaming hands, that I shoved to the floor, is the mayor's wife, I do believe."

Calmed down, we did enjoy our cocoa that I made with cocoa powder, sugar, Jersey milk and a sprinkle of cayenne powder. It was lovely, soothing, and the cayenne warmed the cockles of the heart.

# Chapter 14

As we sipped our cocoa, he told me about his mother. "Dad went back to Scotland to meet her. She was a distant cousin from a remote area. She was very shy, but he convinced her to come. They got married in her village. He had to hold her tight on the plane as she was so scared. She never learned English and this farm allowed her to be reclusive. She was an excellent cook, needlewoman and gardener. Like you, this was the life she loved. Dad was fifty when I was born and she was forty-three. I was a menopause baby and Doc McIntyre delivered me right here at home in the big bed. She died at seventy, when I was twenty-seven. She was quiet and shy, but she had a good sense of humor and I miss her very much."

"I feel her presence even though I never met her—her kitchen, her clothes and aprons, her utensils, her son and yet, I don't feel her as resentful. I even talk to her sometimes. I call her Janet. I sort of think she likes me."

"She liked your brothers very much."

"My brothers?"

"Dennis and Jim came here on their bicycles one Thursday after school. I think they were curious. She brought them in and gave them fruitcake and tea. Dad called your mom to let her know where they were. They all played dominoes. After that, all that year, they came on Thursday for an hour or so. You were in high school and probably didn't know about it."

"No, I didn't."

"Mom thought a lot of those boys and missed them when you all moved away. Do you remember the day you moved, and Dad and I came over to say good-bye?"

"The worst day of my life! Leaving the farm and leaving you. I thought I would never see you again."

"You wouldn't even look at me. I had to come up to you and take your hand to say 'bye'."

"Then you kissed me on the forehead as if I was six. I was so disappointed."

"Disappointed?"

"I was hoping you would say 'don't go, stay and marry me'."

"Sweetheart, you had just turned sixteen. If I had done that, I could have been arrested. You were under age. What would your family have said? I never even thought about you in those terms. I was losing my little sister."

"I know."

"You funny old thing. Is that why you were so devastated? I never knew, but you know, I wonder did my Dad know, because on the way home he said that you were a lovely girl and that I would never meet another girl like you."

"It's come out right though."

"Aye, it sure has."

The next morning after milking, Brian said that this was my home now and I could make any changes I wanted.

"There is something. What do you think about this?" I indicated the long blank wall in the kitchen from the entrance to the spare chair in the corner by the living room doorway.

"See this space here? What if I emptied the china cabinet, could we move it here and put the chair on the other side of the window near the door? It will fit. I measured."

"Sounds okay, then you would have all the good dishes and things in the kitchen, and the china cabinet matches the table and chairs."

"We could use the good dishes for Sunday supper."

"Leaves a big space in the living room on this side of the window."

"I wondered about putting the desk behind the loveseat, so when one of us is at the desk, we are not way over there."

"That would be an improvement, but now you would have a full blank wall, with a window plum in the middle."

"In my father's house are many books. I have all my kid books, teen books, mysteries, classics and novels that have never been out of the boxes. I love books and I just kept adding to my collection, hoping someday I would have a place for them. If we put up shelving, not the expensive stuff, but economical shelving that would be hidden by the books, on both sides of the window, top to bottom, we could put a window seat under the window and over the heat register. I could whip up a seat cushion. Our own library. What do you think?"

"I think it's a great idea. You can point out the books you think I would enjoy. I've never owned a book, just got them out of the library. Your dad used to recommend books to me like Robert Louis Stevenson and Sir Walter Scott. I got the books and read them to Dad. After your family moved away, I asked Miss Addison, the librarian, to help me and she never failed to come up with good reads like H. Rider Haggard and Ellery Queen. I'll measure everything up and price it out on Monday at lunch time."

# Chapter 15

The hens had a great time scuffing up the vegetation in their run. It was time to put them to work. On Monday, I took the four foot high, coated green vinyl fencing out and cut sections seven feet long. I trimmed all the edges so the hens wouldn't poke their eyes out. The seven foot lengths were bent up into a rounded hoops. I cut two four foot by four foot high sections. One, I fixed in place on the hoop to close the end off. The second, I affixed to the other end with plastic ties on one side and a small bungee cord on the other side, creating a gate. These hoods would go over a four foot by four foot bed in the garden. I made five more, then set them all in place over visible mounds that had been the raised beds. To-morrow morning, the "girls" (Brian had his lassies, so I would have my girls) would be working in the garden.

When Brian came home, he brought shelving and he unloaded it into the living room. It was all pre-cut to the correct lengths. There were metal brackets to go in the wall studs and then the shelves rested on them.

I had emptied the china cabinet and the desk during the day. I was able to move the desk and refill it, but the china cabinet wouldn't budge.

On his way to the drive shed, I saw him stop and look at the garden. After milking, he came in and said," The ladies plowing to-morrow, are they?"

"The girls," I corrected. He laughed as he sat down to his meal. "Where did you come up with the pop bottle waterers?"

"At the pet store. They're for cats and were dirt cheap and I scrounged the plastic pop bottles from the garbage at the variety store."

After supper, we moved the china cabinet into the kitchen. I had washed the contents and now packed them back in as he used a stud finder and marked the walls. He used a 'laser' measuring tape to get the right alignment; then he installed the brackets. As soon as he finished one side, I placed the shelves in place. I couldn't reach the top, but went over to the other side when he finished there, and he put the top shelves up. We admired our handiwork, much pleased. He busied himself with his measuring tape getting the dimensions for the window seat.

After work on Friday, Brian brought home a German Shepherd pup so I wouldn't "get lonely in the daytime". We called him "Buster" and he was very well-behaved, not a barker, and seemed intelligent.

# Chapter 16

On Sunday, after church, we drove straight to Mom and Dad's. My brother Jay was home from the university in Virginia.

"Is this the baby? I can't believe it." Brian grabbed Jay's hand and they hugged each other in a bear hug.

"Wow, Brian, I always wondered if you really were as big as I thought you were when I was ten. It's so good to see you and I'm so glad you and Georgie found each other again. We all loved you so much and you were such a part of our childhood."

Jay was big, but not as big as Brian, but tall, athletic and muscular and was a great help in shifting all those boxes of books. I had packed them in smaller boxes as I thought I would be moving them and books are heavy. This resulted in many more trips than bigger boxes would have taken.

Mom would have liked us to stay for supper, but she knew we had to get back for the lassies. She had packed us a box supper with fried chicken, salad, bottles of juice, and an iced icebox cake.

Brian backed into the drive shed. "I'll take your car to-morrow. You and I will work on moving them to-morrow night. Don't you start during the day. I'll bring home the mover's dolly and we'll do it in no time. I should have borrowed it for the weekend."

My girls had six twelve foot beds done and I moved them to the last six beds. They didn't mind being carried and I talked to them as I put them in their "tractor".

After supper, Brian backed the truck up to the door. With the dolly, the boxes were quickly brought in. They were alphabetically labeled and we put them in the approximate place.

"How will you ever reach the top shelf if I'm not here?"

"I'll wait for you. I'm patient. I've waited before."

We couldn't wait for the weekend, but each night we shelved a few boxes.

"This looks good," he would say.

"Oh, Brian, you have to read that!"

He hadn't heard of Clive Cussler, John Grisham, Jack Higgins, and so many other favorites. He may never have to go back to the library again.

The following week, he returned from work with a beautiful maple bench with cross supports. "I road tested it and it will hold me." He'd taken the measurements to a local carpenter and had it made. It fit perfectly under the window. The next day, I purchased a slab of foam and a neutral chintz remnant and made up the cushion.

# Chapter 17

I went picking strawberries at a farm quite a distance from us and got enough berries to put down thirty quarts in the freezer. We were also eating and freezing asparagus every other day.

The girls progressed across the garden. I had gotten the greens in as soon as I came to the farm, and I was planting behind the hens. I weeded out the raspberries and the asparagus bed, and put the girls to work on a long new bed along the north fence. When they were done, I installed a metal weed barrier along the fence, sunk in the ground. This I planted to a new raspberry bed, as we both loved them so much, and they are good for you. The ones on the east fence only produced in June, while the new ones would produce in June and September.

Brian stood looking over the garden gate. "I never would have believed it. What a terrific way to work a garden. I told the guys at work and I don't think they believed me. You're a whiz."

Our life settled into a comfy routine. I painted the henhouse and the pig sty with red barn paint and the trim was white. Brian thought the barn had gone unpainted long enough, but I convinced him to have professional barn painters do it red and white, and to do the drive shed at the same time. The drive shed would be dark brown with white trim. Brian took his one week holiday when they were there.

He traded in my old car for a big, tomato-red, heavy-duty pickup truck. "I was so sick in my heart at the thought of selling the farm, I had decided on a black truck to match my mood, but when I saw this one, I thought that's me and my life now, so I had to have the red one."

"How much did they allow you for the old Topaz?"

"Twenty-two hundred. I'll give you the money."

"Don't be daft. I'd have to turn around and give it to you to pay for the green truck and would the meter be running every time I rode in the truck?"

He just laughed and shook his head. "Georgie, you'll be the death of me."

Finally! He had called me 'Georgie' same as everyone else.

When he came home of a night and I saw that big red truck break through the trees heading up the driveway to the house, my heart sang, "Home is the sailor, home from the sea. Home is the hunter, home from the hill" I paraphrased A.E. Housman.

# Chapter 18

I bought some turned wood legs and wood for frames and painted the legs moss green; made up frames to act as table tops, and painted them green as well. Then the two sets went under the kitchen windows and I placed two long window boxes on the frames. The boxes I planted to pink ivy geraniums, blue ageratum, a yellow marigold, trailing mauve verbena and a potato vine at each corner with their cascading vibrant green leaves. Bracketed by the climbing roses, the picture was complete.

One day I planned a cold supper, took out the tractor and cut the hay field. Brian had argued but I told him he had to stop thinking of me as fragile. "I'm here to make your work easier. Remember?" The weather stayed nice and I turned it the next day. On Saturday, Brian got out the bailer and then we brought it in from the field, sending it up to the mow on the hay elevator. In this climate, drying is not a problem as long as the weather stays hot and dry. The mid-afternoon temperature now was between ninety and one hundred. We drank a lot of mineral water and juice.

I was cleaning out the pig sty while Brian unloaded the last of the load we had picked up that morning. He had his shirt off and his back was towards me.

Brian has no hair on his upper body. He was covered with sweat and as I watched he picked up bales on his left side, torqued his body to the right and sent the bales up the elevator. He looked like a body builder coated in baby oil, as his muscles flexed and rippled. What a wonderful sight he was! I went back to work. I was filled with pride, but knew if I ever said anything he would be most embarrassed. We were a shy pair of birds.

Brian gave me a hummingbird feeder, hummingbird swing and a wrought iron shepherd's hook for my birthday. We installed it outside the screened porch on the north side where we were spending more time as it was cool there. One night, when we lingered admiring the full moon, the fields leading up to the mountain were bathed in light, and then out from the trees came a herd of ten or twelve deer. It was absolutely magical.

One evening, we were sitting on a bench Brian had made and put by the barn door. "Were you ever lonely when you were going to college, or did you have lots of friends?"

"I've been lonely since I was sixteen. When you carried me down the hay mow ladder and set me down, you noticed I was flushed and so I was. I'd just been struck by lightning.

That lightning was you. I knew right then and there I would love you forever. When we moved when I was sixteen, I was rudderless for a while and then I threw myself into my studies and I got my job and that kept me from thinking about you. I knew I would never marry, because it wouldn't be fair to lead some person to think they could ever be number one in my heart. That place was taken. Loneliness was just an ache I had to live with. How about you?"

"I've been lonely since the day I was born. An only child of elderly parents living apart from other people. I thought it would go away when I went to school. It didn't. I was head and shoulders taller than the other kids and big in my body. They called me 'Jumbo' and sometimes 'Dumbo'. I hated it. When we played baseball, I hit it over the fence most times and then someone would have to climb the fence and go searching in Cecil Patterson's corn field for the ball. Soon they wouldn't let me hit anymore. I heard more swear words on the first day of school than my father had heard in a lifetime. He complained but the teacher said they couldn't be responsible for the language used in the homes. She sent a letter out but of course it did no good.

The only time I didn't have the ache was when I was with your family. By then, I was out of school and started on the roads, when I was seventeen. At your place, your dad challenged my mind and opened me up intellectually to books, music, art, politics, theology and philosophy. Your Gran was very loving to me. I think she knew how desperately lonely and shy I was. Your mom always had a tea and a dessert for me. You and your brothers could make me laugh. You were the siblings I never had. I was only happy at your place. After you moved away, the ache was back but I learned to put it on the back burner because your dad taught me to amuse and challenge myself. I never needed or wanted friends. The guys I work with are just people I spend part of my days with. Tom, the mechanic is friendly, but he has his own worries— his wife has just left him."

In bed one night, I rolled into him and he wrapped his arms around me.

"Sweetheart, I'm thinking of buying you a gun."

"A gun! I'll shoot myself, or you, or the dog, or the windows. I don't want a gun. Whatever for?"

"I'm away all day. You're here alone. I worry about you. I'll teach you gun safety and how to shoot. It'll be fun. You'll see. You can practice every day, then just put it loaded in the top drawer of the cupboard by the door. I'll just feel better. Humor me, please."

I argued and dug in my toes, but home he came one day with a small revolver, not automatic. We had a little practice every day and slowly fewer and fewer tin cans and pop bottles were surviving the onslaught.

"You do know I could never shoot anyone no matter what."

"It's just a precaution. Don't fret. Just put it in the drawer. Forget it."

Our summer was very productive. We canned, pickled and froze. I made endless plastic containers of spaghetti sauce. The jars on the shelves in the basement and the freezer were filling up. Every Sunday, we laid out produce in paper sacks for people to take home from church with them. We delivered carrots and potatoes to the local food bank. We had also built up our stores in the pantry. We didn't make jam or jelly as it contained too much sugar. Janet hadn't either for the same reason. "The only jam I ever tasted was your Gran's Plum and Apple Jam and it was wonderful on a hot biscuit." We had bags of asparagus, strawberries, raspberries, three kinds of beans, blackberries, blueberries, peaches, cherries, broccoli, and whole small tomatoes in the freezer. We were eating out of the garden—stir frying, sautéing, steaming, baking and eating raw. We felt well all the time and we were tanned and muscled.

In the evenings we read, danced, watched sports, listened to CDs, or sang.

On Sunday evenings, my resident Scot played the bagpipes. I sat in the screened porch with the dog beside me with his head on my knee, while Brian played so beautifully, sometimes it would almost make you cry.

# Chapter 19

One morning in November, a strange car came up the driveway at a rapid pace and stopped outside the door. I went out. A young man in a tee shirt and work pants shouted, "Are you Georgia?" I said I was. "Come with me. There's been an accident. Brian's hurt."

I tore my apron off, went in the house and threw it over the back of my chair, grabbed my purse and locked the door behind me.

"I'll take the truck."

"No. Come with me, now. I was told to bring you."

"By whom?"

"Brian."

I got in and we turned around at the barn and sped away to town.

"I'm Tom. I work with Brian."

"Oh, you're the truck mechanic at the Public Works."

"Yes ma'am. Brian was helping me and that young bast . . . sorry ma'am, that idiot turned the key on."

"You better tell me calmly what happened."

Brian had been helping Tom with a repair, which he frequently did, as Tom had no assistant. They were repairing a dump truck engine with the hood up. They completed the repair and tightened the fan shroud. Tom stepped back and Brian was doing the same when some young man who worked in the office and had been banned from even going in the fenced off compound yard, had climbed up in the cab, saw Tom step clear, didn't know Brian was under there, and turned the key on. The fan sliced Brian's left hand off at the wrist.

"A second earlier, he would have cut his head off." Tears were pouring down Tom's face.

"Did they get the hand?"

"Yes, they took it with them in the ambulance. It was cut off cleanly, not mangled. Brian was conscious and yelled at me to come and get you. He said, 'Don't let her drive. She will be all shook up'."

I was all shook up and in shock. I locked my hands to stop the shaking. "Brian, Brian", I was screaming in my mind. "Oh, my beautiful Brian."

We rushed into emergency. I had to sign some papers—I had no idea what, then we were whisked to a waiting room outside the operating theater. It was a long, long time later that the doctor came out to us.

"Mrs. MacKenzie, we were able to re-attach the hand, but time will tell if the body rejects it or not. We got the hand quickly and did the operation which is certainly in his favor. Would you like some medication to get you through to-night and to-morrow?"

"No, thanks, I don't take medication. Can I see him?"

"He's still unconscious."

"Can I sit by him until he comes to?"

"It could be some time."

"Do you have his truck keys?"

"I would presume so."

"I'll drive his truck home, Tom. I need to milk the cows and then I'll come back. I'll stay the night, if I can, Doctor?"

"Of course. I'll speak to the head nurse and she'll look after you."

"Are you sure you are alright to drive?"

"I'll be okay, Tom, and thank you for bringing me and telling me what happened, and also for waiting with me."

A nurse brought me Brian's keys, his wallet and a white sealed envelope. I could tell by the bulge what it was.

Tom ferried me back to the yard. As I got in the truck, I heard Tom tell an older man, "They attached the hand, but they don't know if it will take or not. Where's that flaming kid?"

"Don't worry. Daddy came and got him."

I drove home very carefully. Brian wouldn't want to know I wrecked his new truck.

The lassies were used to me helping with the milking so gave me no grief, but they kept watching the door. When I let them out in the barnyard, they lined up along the fence by the drive. There was the truck! Where was he? At night, they just went in the barnyard, otherwise, in the morning you would have to round them up, traipsing through long, dewy grass.

I had a strong cup of tea to fortify myself and then I packed a bag for Brian, tucked my nightgown and undies in my purse with a toothbrush and paste. I put Brian's keys, wallet and envelope in his cuff-link box.

At the hospital, I sat on his right side as there were monitors, tubes and things on his left side which was elevated above his heart and disappeared into a mound of bandages.

The staff checked in every once in a while and each time offered to bring me anything I wanted. At nine-thirty, they wheeled in a cot with a big fluffy mattress. Quickly it was made up for me. They had already shown me where the bathroom was. A chrome handle on the wall, when turned, opened a door revealing a toilet and sink in a miniscule room. If they hadn't shown me the handle, I would never have known it was there. The cafeteria, they pointed out,was just down the hall and to the left, but at this time of night was now closed, but there were vending machines. I assured them I was fine.

I brushed my teeth, combed my hair and put on my nightgown that had been Janet's, said my prayers, and climbed in the cot. It took a long time to go sleep.

"Georgie." It was a whisper, but I was instantly awake and at his side. His right arm curled around me.

"I'm here, mo chridhe".*

"I knew you would be. What are we going to do about the lassies?"

"They're milked, but they can't figure out where you are. I left them lined up along the fence looking at your truck."

"We need to get someone in to help. Maybe Ian Ferguson can lend us his hired man. We'd pay, of course."

Ian Ferguson was the elderly neighbor next to us down the road.

"If you are talking about that red-haired hired hand, I don't think you would rest easy knowing he was on the farm."

"He does have a reputation among the woman."

"I hear he's very aggressive and doesn't believe no means no. I'd have my gun trained on him with the safety off the whole time. No. We are fine. I may take longer that you, but I'll 'getter done', as they say."

---

* "mo Chridhe" - Scottish Gaelic for "my Heart/ "my Love".

He drifted off to sleep again and I eased out of his arm and went back to the cot. They gave him a shot at three a.m. At four-thirty, I got up, washed, dressed and left the hospital.

After milking, letting the cows out to the pasture, and cleaning the barn, I showered, dressed and had a good cup of tea, a muffin and a banana. I put a few tea bags in a plastic bag in my purse. Perhaps the cafeteria could give me a pot of hot water so we could have good tea together. Buster watched me with a mournful look.

Suddenly, I felt overwhelmed. What if he had to have a hook or an artificial limb? How would he cope? I sat there blubbering, "Why, God?" Then I stopped. Don't say that! Don't ever say that! What you mean is why did this happen to us? Why not to someone else? What a nasty, selfish thought. It happened to us and we would cope. God doesn't give you more burden than you can handle. "We will cope with your help and guidance. Make us strong in the face of adversity." I prayed. "Thy will be done."

That afternoon, my parents came over and Brian cheered to see them.

"We have a surprise for you."

My older brother, Mick, stepped in the door. Brian was so glad to see him. Mick is two years older than me, while the other boys are all younger. Mick had been Brian's shadow anytime he was at our place. They greeted each other as enthusiastically as they could.

Mick explained, "I'm just back from Afghanistan and I want to stay at your place and do the farm work while you are laid up."

Brian was reluctant to say what needed doing, as he is a very proud man.

"Brian, I need peace and quiet. You would be doing me a very great favor if you have lots for me to do, and you will not pay me." He and Brian went over the fall schedule.

I took Mick home with me. What an answer to a prayer he was! Thank you, God. He knew all about milking machines and farm work as two years older than me, he farmed until he was eighteen. I whipped up a meal.

"This place is paradise, Georgie. No loud noises. I'm off for three months."

Next day, the doctor told us the hand was warm, had a pulse and the levels of potassium in the blood returning from the hand was favorable. Time would tell.

Each day he improved. Alex had been in several times, as had Tom, who finally stopped looking so scared. He brought a card from the men.

Five days later, the Manager of Public Works showed up for a visit. He was a heavy-set man, sweating profusely (in November?) and seemed fidgety.

"Well, Brian, I hear you're doing remarkably well. Everyone misses you, of course. Oh, hello. Mrs. MacKenzie, is it? How are you?"

"Fine, thanks." Who did he think I was—a camp-follower?

"Now Brian, you are not to worry about a thing. The insurance will pay for everything, including whatever therapy you might need. There is a downside, however. Your therapy could take months they tell me, so we are going to have to replace you. We can't keep your job open that long. Of course, there will be two week's severance pay—oh, my—that was a poor choice of words."

My eyes had narrowed down to slits as I looked at him through my eyelashes.

"Of course, there's your pension that you may be able to tap into, considering the circumstances. Now you take care and I'll try to look in again sometime." He turned and literally fled from the room. I was right behind him.

"Georgie . . . ."

"Shh, I'll get tea." I crept out the door. As I peered down the hall, the manager turned into the cafeteria. I hurried to the doorway, but before I could enter, I heard a raspy voice say," Well, how'd it go?"

"He never said a word. Just lay there looking at me. It's hard to see a big man like that laid low."

"It was an accident and accidents happen."

"I didn't like the look of his missus. She looked mean."

"Georgie McGee? A stupid farm girl from the back roads. She won't make any trouble. If she does, I can get four or five good old boys to say she was always fast and just looking for a meal ticket, that's why she latched onto MacKenzie."

"He's a decent fellow and well liked."

"Yeah, yeah, but he's just a dumb Scotch-American. Hell, his parents didn't even speak English."

"What language did they speak?"

"Oh, some garbled Scotch lingo."

They sounded like they were moving away from me. I stepped around the corner. The second voice belonged to the mayor—the "Boss Hog" of our town.

I went back to the room. "Where's the tea?"

"I'll get some later. My instincts told me to follow the manager. I kept out of sight, but guess who he was reporting to."

"Not the mayor."

I looked at Brian in surprise. "Bingo."

# Chapter 20

"The kid that turned the key was the mayor's seventeen year old son. His dad parachuted him into a job at the Public Works. He's supposed to work in the office. He's a smart aleck—you know the type—'I'm the mayor's son and I can do whatever I want'. Two days after he arrived, he wrecked the yard ATV at lunch time. That's when they banned him from setting foot in the compound."

"And you and Tom were doing repairs in the compound?"

"That's right."

"We need legal advice, Brian. Don't sign anything. Not insurance papers, release papers.—nothing. I'll call Dad. He'll know what to do. He'll speak to Reuben."

"Who's Reuben?"

"The lawyer for the company where Dad works. Reuben takes care of everything legal. He and Dad are very good friends."

I phoned Dad from home, when I knew he would still be at the office. I told him most of what I knew. He told me to sit tight and someone would call me. An hour and fifteen minutes later, Steve Rappaport, Reuben's son, called me from Charlotte where he had a law office. He told me he would meet us at the hospital the next morning at ten o'clock.

I made supper for Mick, who had been finishing up the plowing all day, and then I went back to the hospital. Brian and I had supper together. I brought our meal in our picnic basket, and had got hot water from the cafeteria for our tea. Just fruit for dessert, as Brian had to watch his calories as he was getting no exercise.

The next morning at five to ten, Steve introduced himself. He was a short, thin fellow with a marvelous smile. He got out a small tape recorder and had Brian tell him all about the accident, how the mayor's underage son was responsible, and how he had been told of his termination.

"Firstly, let's refer to this from now on as a 'reckless act'. Secondly, how cruel to terminate you like that. A lesser man would have already been in a deep depression over the anxiety of the hand."

He recorded exactly what I did and heard.

"How long has this mayor been in office? He sounds like a real dictator."

"Seems like forever, and he will be as long as he wants. He keeps a squad of goons and red-necks who should be in jail, to intimidate and terrorize people. The election turn-out is less than twenty percent. Why bother? It's said he has his fingers in many pies and has lots of friends in low places."

"I love taking on these big frogs in little ponds. The 'Boss Hog' type is meat and gravy to me."

"I have to tell you about Georgie. She gave me a copy of a doctor's examination she had two days before we got married. She wanted to be sure she didn't have any serious condition that would be a drain on our finances." Steve looked at me sharply. "Yes, isn't she something? Who, but Georgia would even think of such a thing. On that paper, it indicated that she was a virgin, so if the mayor thinks he can besmirch her name, he has another think coming."

"Wow! Hang onto that paper. If he tries those tricks, that paper could be worth a lot of money. Is there anything else that could factor in if we file a lawsuit against the mayor, his son, and or the County?"

"Well, there is something," I murmured, "and I'm not sure, but I just missed a second period and I think I may be pregnant, but I haven't done the test yet."

"What?"

"I'm sorry, Brian, but it's just maybe." His right arm went around me.

"Take that test to-day, Georgia. It's added responsibility for Brian and has to factor in for expenses in the future. Brian, are you looking for your old job back or another job with the County? They should have offered you alternative employment. How long have you worked for them.?"

"Fourteen years—never sick, never late. I took two hours off to get our marriage license. That's it, but no, I don't want my job or any job. Look at my wife. Isn't she lovely? I suffered every day since we got married, thinking of her home alone. Everyone knows I'm gone from seven in the morning until five-thirty in the evening. Every time I hear on the radio about a woman kidnapped, raped, beaten or killed, I start to sweat. It could be my Georgie. I got her a German shepherd dog and a gun trying to protect her, but still I worry."

"Oh, Brian." I felt like crying, thinking of him worrying every day.

"Anything else?"

"Well, if you are thinking about laying any charges or whatever against the kid, you better be aware that he could disappear. There's an older brother and the mayor forced him on the office staff at city hall. One evening, just after the Daylight Savings went off in the fall of last year, it was quite dim out when the workday finished. He tried to rape one of the young secretaries, in the parking lot. One of the other girls coming out the front door heard the screams, alerted staff and one of them called 911. The poor girl was in a bad way, with her slacks yanked down and ripped. Her nose was broken; her lips were split and she ended up with two black eyes. He had beaten her to try to get what he wanted. Police arrived at the mayor's house. The mayor and his wife were so concerned as Robbie hadn't phoned or come home. His truck was located later in the Wal-Mart parking lot, and no one has seen hide nor hair of him since, but there is still a warrant out for his arrest. The girl left the state, as she and her family were afraid of the mayor intimidating her to change her story. Apparently, her cousin told me, she is quite prepared to return to testify if they ever get him to court."

"What a sordid family. You've given me lots to think about."

"Steve, how do we pay you? Retainer up front?" I asked.

"You don't pay me a cent. I get ten percent of whatever I get for you, either in court or by settlement."

After Steve left, we talked about the possible forthcoming baby—what all we had to do to get ready for such an arrival. Brian was over the moon.

# Chapter 21

I took the test and I was pregnant which buoyed Brian's spirits.

"First thing, I've got to get out of here. We have plans to make and things to do for this baby. Oh, Georgia, this is the best news a man could get. I'll jump through all their hoops, so I can get home."

Brian's body had accepted the re-attached hand, but he had to wear a brace to support the tendons. At last his arm was lowered, and they were getting him up each day. Mild therapy was started which would intensify as he progressed, but we were told it could take a year or more before he would have eighty to ninety percent usage of the hand. Even so, he was thankful to the Lord and to his surgeon and he thanked both every chance he could.

Alex was a frequent visitor and when Brian finally came home, we invited Alex to join us for Sunday supper and to give the three of us communion. I cooked a rump roast with mashed potatoes, mashed turnip with butter and a touch of maple syrup, and coleslaw. Dessert was apple pie.

"You cook old country style," Alex remarked. I haven't tasted this kind of cooking since I left Scotland. My mother was a terrific cook, like you Georgia. I have her recipe for a steamed pudding with plumped, rum-soaked raisins in it. I have translated it to American measures but no one is interested."

"I would love to have it. I promise I to make it and you shall have it for dessert next time."

"Don't misunderstand me. I've had some lovely meals in this country, but the southern fare is different from British meals"

"I know what you mean. My Gran taught my mother and me to cook, so we cook north England style, plus we cook American and Southern, but chicken is the chosen meat of North Carolina, while beef is the British choice. Other days of the week, we eat kale, collards and mustard greens, but not on Sunday. Brian's mother cooked the old country way too, so he was raise on the same kind of foods as we were."

"We Presbyterians have no ban on alcohol like the Baptists?" asked Mick.

"Scottish Presbyterians invented whiskey and the church wouldn't have lasted five minutes if a ban had been imposed on their industry, but what was said and what we adhere to is 'all things in moderation'."

After the meal, I refused all help and shooed them out to enjoy the afternoon sun while it lasted. The nights were cold and frosty, but the sun shone and the temperature rose in the daytime.

Alex was asking Mick about his service in Afghanistan, as I came out and sat on the bench, to the right of Brian.

"I'm dreading going back. Being here on this farm has been such a respite for me. I have one more tour of duty, but Afghanistan again is too much. I've been there five years and have seen too much; lost too many friends, and been wounded too many times—none of them seriously however, but, when does one's luck run out? I'm thinking of absconding to Canada. I hate to shirk my duty, but I've lost my nerve which will make me a liability. It's sickening me."

"Why don't you petition for alternate placement? Ask for a psychological evaluation, if you have to. I'll give you a letter recommending a change. I'm a padre, so it may carry some weight. To change the subject, do you remember Patsy Bannister, Mick? She's just returned home from medical school and is looking for a job. You and she were pretty good friends, if I remember right. I recall different occasions when one or other of you complained how you hated the other. Patsy once said you put a frog down the back of her dress at choir practice, and you complained that she lied and told the teacher you called her bad names. When a boy and girl express that much animosity, it's usually a sign of interest. She's a little down in the dumps—all that education and no job. She's a bit of an environmentalist, so you have something in common."

"Old Patsy Bannister! How come she isn't married?"

"Too busy studying and working, trying to keep ahead of her student loans."

"Old Patsy Bannister!"

"She's the same age as you, old Mick." I observed dryly.

Time moved along, with long sessions of therapy both at the clinic and at home, but Brian worked hard, never fudging on what was expected of him. He was determined to have one hundred percent rehabilitation. Mick got a letter from Alex, and he did look up "Old Patsy" and they got along like a house on fire. For his last tour of duty, Mick was posted to Italy. Alex married them in January, and they went to Italy in March. As a married man, Mick was allowed to live off the base.

Before they left, Mick told us how staying in our little paradise had helped him mentally and when this tour was over, they wanted to buy a farm somewhere and put down roots, preferably in a place where Patsy could put her medical training to use.

# Chapter 22

Our lawsuit against the mayor, his son and the county was progressing. Steve told us people were calling him with horror stories about the treatment they had received from "His Honor". They didn't want to bother us as they knew Brian was in therapy to gain mobility of his hand, but they wanted us to know they cared.

Brian had a real hang-up about his hand. He would never put his left arm around me and avoided touching me with his left hand. We didn't dance anymore. I just let it be, not wanting to make him more touchy about it.

Mick had finished the fields we had selected to bring under cultivation. One field under the mountain had a stream running through the corner. Brian had repaired the fencing and put in a water trough, piping the stream in and out of the trough, before his accident. That stream, like so many in the mountain area, never dried up but ran beautiful pure spring water downstream all year round. We planned to raise young Black Angus calves to maturity starting in the spring. I suggested we buy an all-terrain vehicle (ATV) to get around the property. Brian agreed that would facilitate things like cruising the woods, and taking salt licks and hay to the steers.

During winter, we inventoried the woods. The cold bothered Brian's hand badly, so we bought him a wool pea jacket and I removed the left pocket. I knitted him a pair of angora mitts. Now he could put his mitted hand into the pocket and rest it against the warmth of his body. We methodically worked those woods. Brian was very knowledgeable about the type of trees growing there. We took a section, he called out the numbers of the varieties; I recorded those numbers, noting what needed to be removed.

We contacted the Department of Agriculture. They told us we had to have at least ten acres agricultural, five acres horticulture and twenty acres of forestry. Once we told them we exceeded all those levels they became very interested and representatives came to the farm one day. We laid out our plans and they told us what was expected of us. We could qualify for a lower tax rate on the worked farm and forest; we had to replant harvested trees according to the management program they set us; tax would be deferred indefinitely as long as the property continued to qualify for the program.

"How will you do all the planting and work while you are being rehabilitated?"

"We plan to hire agricultural students to help us with the manual part that can't be done mechanically. Also, we plan to use a system to get two and three crops off a field—the last crop being red clover and timothy, so that when the field is cut, it would be at rest the next year and become a pasture." Brian showed the gentlemen an article about a farmer in Denton who is getting four crops a year off a farm.

"What is it you plan to grow in this field—this one marked 'mangel/carrot?

I told him about the animal food supplements used in Europe.

"I think you better show these fellows your qualifications," suggested Brian.

I got out my certificates and they seemed to be impressed.

"We know of a brother and sister that live quite near here. They are both in Ag. college, and plan to resurrect their father's acreage to make it more productive. They could help you with your planting and learn as they go. Can I give you their names? They only live about five miles from here but in the next county. They are African-Americans? Do you have a problem with that?"

"Absolutely not. If we have to be hyphenated, we are Scottish-Americans. Hope they don't mind. Sounds like a perfect set-up. Georgie wants to plant a strawberry field as you see on our plan and we will need to get on with it if we want to capture the market next year. My brother-in-law and I worked all the fields you see marked in red. We have to get started as they need attention before the spring rains bring the weeds."

We signed and they left us our copy of the agreement and brochures on obtaining non-genetically modified seed for corn, potatoes and soybeans. Also, how to have your farm certified as organic. We were interested in corn, but for eating not cattle food. They wrote down the phone number for the young farmers-to-be.

We had oats and alfalfa to plant as well, so we made up a schedule for the work. I called Marty and Ben and we made an appointment for them to come and see us. Luckily, they had a car they used for commuting to school.

When they arrived, Buster went nuts over them. We sat around the table with tea and shortbread. We showed them the plans, time schedule, equipment on hand, and crop lists, plus Brian asked me to show them my credentials as he insisted I was to be the orchestra leader on this project, and he said he and they would follow my instructions. This made me a little nervous—if it all went pear-shaped, we would all know who to blame, wouldn't we?

Our great adventure was starting. I loved having Brian home full time, and he loved being there. His heart had always belonged to the land.

# Chapter 23

The orchard, we had partitioned off from a field. The orchard part would be the pig field. We sprayed the fruit trees with a new organic mixture called "Surround"—a clay compound that confounds pests. It was non-toxic and would not harm the new piglets when they were released from the sty and pen and housed in their little Quonset huts and free-ranging.

Our flock of hens was much enlarged and a health food store nearby was taking all the eggs we could produce. One of the first hens got broody and sat on her eggs, adding more eggs each day. We wanted to enlarge the flock even more, so we bought a box of ten chicks, sexed so all were female. That night, Brian and I entered the henhouse after dark. Brian held the flashlight and the little carton of chicks. I lifted the hen, removed the old eggs to a little pail, set her almost all the way back down, but first chick after chick went under the drowsy hen until all ten were nestled under her. We left and dumped the old eggs in the pig run. In the morning at daybreak, what a commotion from the henhouse! We let the hens out as it was rather warm. The hen cackled and strutted, proudly showing off her chicks. The other hens were most appreciative. This was an old trick of Gran's when she wanted to introduce a new breed to the chicken yard. The new chicks were Rhode Island Reds. So now we could distinguish between the old hens and the young ones, for culling purposes.

We planned to put up a rough shelter and run for cockerels that we would raise for two months or so for meat sales.

We kept the girls moving. When they weren't in the garden doing their tractor duties, they were in a large dog pen with a water bottle, and a tarp over one end for shade. Wherever we put the run down, they weeded.

One day was a shocker—the girls caught a snake—a copperhead, something we were vigilantly watching for as they poisonous and aggressive. The hen swung that thing in the air, then, all were jumping to peck off a hunk. The hen in possession ran with the snake fluttering out behind her like an evil banner. In short order, the snake was gone. "Make sure those eggs go somewhere. I don't want one," Brian stated firmly. I didn't fancy one either. For a couple of days the pigs benefited.

In April, Steve came to the farm. He had received notice of when the trial would begin and he wanted to tell us in person. He went crazy over the farm, and for a city-boy, he was very knowledgeable, then he told us his grandparents farmed outside Syracuse, New York, and he spent every summer on that farm growing up.

We told him we were all organic, and he told us, he and his wife ate natural as much as possible.

"Have you heard of 'Kerrygold' butter from Ireland? Costs twice as much as our pound of butter because it's from grass-fed cows. The same with the cheese that comes from Switzerland and Holland. You should look into a farm dairy. Think of real ice cream, not that fake gelatinous stuff we get from the stores. There's a farm dairy near Julian and their ice cream if terrific. Take a jaunt over there. They're very friendly. They'll share the pitfalls and successes with you, I'm sure. Mention my name and Cindy's. You are far enough away not to be competition to them.

This is your Garden of Eden. So beautiful and exactly what a farm should look like, but I see what you meant about Georgia being isolated. The elevation and the surrounding trees make this a world apart. If it wasn't for the planes flying going to Charlotte, you would think you were back in time."

# Chapter 24

A week before the trial was to start, I was washing the breakfast dishes and Brian was still in the barn, when a big, black car with shaded windows came barreling through the trees and up the driveway at a high rate of speed, went passed the house and stopped in the barnyard.

I ran out the French doors, through the screened porch, behind the garden where the new raspberries were shoulder high, behind the chicken house and run, behind the pig sty and run, behind the drive shed. From the corner to the door of the dairy was only a few yards. I went into the dairy where the blinds were closed and it was cool and dark. The door into the barn had a window in it. I could hear shouting from the barn. Through the window, I could see two chubby guys in black suits had Brian pinned against the wall. One man was holding a knife. Just then the other man punched Brian in the stomach and he buckled over, but the same man yanked Brian upright by the hair, as I silently moved into the barn. The lassies were mooing at the upset.

"If you don't withdraw that law suit to-day, we'll be back, and next time we'll let you watch what we do your wife."

"I hear she's a looker," sneered the knife holder.

Brian and I made eye contact. I raised the gun, wavered, then shot the ceiling. The cows jerked and the two men jumped. Brian grabbed both in head locks and slammed their heads together. They dropped like a ton of bricks and the knife flew across the floor.

Pointing the gun at the floor, I flew to Brian "I didn't have to shoot them. I didn't have to shoot them, Brian." Tears streamed down my face. He took the gun in his right hand and gathered me to him with his left arm, his left hand cradling my forearm.

"Shhh, sweetheart. You did wonderful! What a girl, but we have to call 911."

"I already did when I saw them come through the trees. I knew they were trouble. I told the dispatcher we had intruders and they had gone to barn to kill you, so I imagine we'll have lots of company."

"I hear vehicles coming now, but what is Buster barking at? Is he tied up?"

Suddenly the dairy door and the barn door flew open and we had a SWAT team in our barn! They advanced on us, automatic guns leveled. Their huge black helmets made them look like Martians or black carpenter ants. They moved closer.

It was very scary. Brian snapped the safety on and dropped the gun. Uniformed officers flooded in, followed by a tall older man in a brown suit who came up to us.

"What happened here, Brian?"

Brian told him and when he mentioned I shot the gun, all eyes swiveled to look at the ceiling.

"Great shot, Mrs. M.," one young officer chuckled.

Brian finished off the story as we moved towards the barn doorway.

"Brian, can you call your dog off?" Another young officer by the black car called. Buster was still barking furiously and snarling at the back seat of the car. We could just see his legs under the passenger's door. Brian whistled and Buster came bounding towards us, tail wagging and long red tongue lolling out the side of his mouth. Brian patted him.

The ambulance crew went by with the two black suits on gurneys. Apparently, they were badly concussed. A uniformed officer was pulling the mayor out of the back seat of the car, while another applied handcuffs. They patted him down and removed a gun. They frog—marched him to a police car.

The young officer who had called about Buster came up to us.

"That's some dog you have there. The mayor was trying to get to the front seat to escape, but your dog assumed the canine 'hold' position. He had his hackles up, front legs planted stiff, lips curled, snarling and barking. The mayor couldn't even reach the door handle to close the door."

We bent down to thank Buster properly. He slurped us royally.

"You have a wonderful farm here, Brian," the older man observed, "but what are all those little steel huts in the orchard with the pigs?"

We explained and said how everything was organically grown.

"Organic, eh? My wife has me eating only organically grown fruit and vegetables. So your garden is organic, too."

"It's a good thing Brian had finished milking or we would have been up to our necks in organic clotted cream," I said. Brian went to let the cows out.

"Why are there chickens in a dog run on the side of the drive?"

"To protect them from hawks and vultures while they are weeding. We move the run every day to give them fresh material."

Brian came up to us, and added, 'You should see them in the evening.

Georgie lets them out and then she walks to the chicken house, calling 'widdy—widdy', and they march along behind her like a Girl Scout troop."

"Why would they do that?"

"They know I'm taking them home where there is food waiting, roosts and safety. Same needs as everything else."

As we walked to the vehicles, the gentleman in brown said quietly, "Brian, I want you to know unofficially that the whole county is hoping you are successful in nailing the mayor to the wall. He is corrupt, nasty, and lots of people have been hurt by him. They are hoping you will expose him. This little caper here to-day is going in the books as an attempted murder and will give us some leeway to look into his affairs."

"That was a good piece of shooting, Mrs. MacKenzie, and you got the job done," commented the chief of police.

I turned to Brian. "I told you I could never shoot anyone, but I was wrong. I was going to shoot them both, but my hand was shaking so bad, I was afraid I would shoot you, so I shot up instead."

"Worked out great this way, love."


Everyone cleared out. Buster sat on the patio and watched them leave. We went into the house. Brian made it as far as the first chair and collapsed. He gathered me into his arms and I sat on his knees. He wrapped his arms around me and the "bump".

We sat for quite some time until we finally calmed down. At the time of attack, we both kept our cool, but when it was all over, we felt quite unstrung. "I better call Steve."

I took his left hand in mine. It looked perfectly normal, no swelling whatsoever, and kissed the back of it. "I'll make tea."

# Chapter 25

On the speaker phone, Steve was very excited about our news. He shared that he was just going to call and warn us as he'd had a call this morning. "This chap told me that he had joked around that he was going to run for mayor. One evening, the doorbell rang and when he opened the door, there were two stout men in black suits, with black fedoras, and darkened sunglasses. They looked like the 'Blues Brothers'. They just stared at him and when he went to close the door, one stuck his foot in and slammed the door open. Just then the mayor got out of the back seat of a big, black car and strolled to the door. "You have a nice little family," said the mayor. The family dog, a Jack Russell, ran up barking and jumping around. The one goon took out a handgun fitted with a long silencer and shot the dog dead right there in the hall. 'I'd consider all your options carefully,' growled the mayor and he sauntered off to the car. The goons followed. The whole family was traumatized as they buried the dog in the backyard. This happened three years ago and they have never told a soul until this morning. He wanted me to warn you. We are dealing with a dangerous man."

After I set out the tea things, I placed the white envelope I had retrieved from his cuff-link box, by his saucer. Brian opened it and shook out his wedding ring.

"Will you do the honors," he whispered.

I whispered back. "With this ring, I thee wed, again."

The next day, Steve called to tell us the case had been put on hold for two months for evidence gathering.

We were interested in the case, but life got in the way. In June, our baby was born. We named him James Angus MacKenzie after his two grandfathers, but we called him "Jam", with the thought that he would grow into "Jamie", when he was older.

# Chapter 26

What a size he was and what a lusty voice he had, demanding attention. When we got him home, Buster went into a frenzy. He adored the baby and would go round in circles to see him. As the baby grew and could focus, the baby loved that dog and was fascinated with him. Brian toted Jam to the barn and set him down in his carrier. Buster, the best babysitter in the world, lay down beside him and didn't move while the baby cooed, gurgled and twitched his feet in the air in delight as he watched the dog's every move.

The lassies seemed very interested in this new little being. Brian carried Jam to each cow and introduced him. The lassies ever go gently, sniffed him.

Now that Brian was over touching me with his left hand, we were back to dancing. Janet had a long black dress with a full skirt. Brian never remembered seeing her wear it. I ruched up the back into a frill, and made a salmon-pink tulle full-skirted petticoat, that peeped out when we twirled. Jam, in his carrier on the desk top, watched with great interest and drummed his heels with glee.

Steve called one day and told us it was all over. The mayor agreed to settle the lawsuit out of court. "The police have been combing through his affairs. Seems he is the sole owner of a casino in West Virginia; sole owner of a tanning salon-spa that is a front for a house of ill repute in Tennessee, and many iffy and illegal projects. Ours was the only lawsuit filed and he didn't want an extensive list of people parading forward and perhaps giving evidence that would get him indicted for more crimes. Our cheque is notarized and I will pick it up at the courthouse. By the way, his older son was arrested in West Virginia, and has been returned in handcuffs, awaiting the attempted rape case."

"It was never about the money," Brian told me when he hung up." I wanted the mayor and his family to take responsibility for their actions, plus how dare he even suggest he could besmirch your reputation. How many other girls have been ruined by those tactics?"

"We are doing great without the County paycheck."

It was true. We had the agreement with the Department of Agriculture and with the Department of Forestry and with the local lumber company, who were clearing out our downfalls, dead wood and diseased trees, opening up the forest for better air flow. The Ag college had a list of students for the replanting of the trees. The cost of the saplings and the labor would be covered under the same program I worked under, when I went north. We would provide facilities and lunch.

Brian contacted a local fellow who was just starting up in the portable toilet business called "Johnny Pot" and he would bring in a portable toilet with washing capabilities, with just one day's notice.

I ran an ad in the local newspaper every week telling what we would have available on Saturday. The garden was providing greens and vegetables. No strawberries this year, as it takes a year for the plants to mature properly. We had contacted the Health Department and had our kitchen inspected, gaining a 98.0 rating, provided I used an extra dishpan for the third sink, which I did.

Our free-range pigs and bulls were all spoken for and deposits taken. Our local butcher, Mr. Ramsay, gave Brian a tour of his slaughterhouse and butcher shop. He assured Brian that he and his son used as humane methods as they could. He couldn't understand people who abused the animals. "Every slash or bash shows up in the meat, you know. We use a moving conveyor belt to move the animal in. The door closes. The conveyor stops. A silenced pistol is inserted in the ear as the animal is patted to calm him down and then we shoot. The conveyor moves the animal off the killing floor and into the back section, out of sight of the next animal."

We were raising six Black Angus steers. One would go to Mr. Ramsay to cover his costs. One would be for us. The other four were sold in sides. A side resulted in approximately two hundred and twenty-five pounds of wrapped and flash frozen meat, delivered. We had a brochure that told of the health benefits of grass-fed, no corn, no antibiotic, no growth hormones beef; the freezer capacity needed and the favorable costs of this meat compared to store-bought meat of unknown origin and treatment. Steve and his wife, Cindy took one side and Cindy's parents took the other side.

Brian and I purchased an all-purpose seed drill and on Saturdays, Ben seeded mangels in one half of a field and carrots in the other half. He planted two rows of purple-top turnips around the perimeter.

We had been to Marty and Ben's parent's farm and while the men and Marty walked the farm, I visited with Mahalia. Soon we were swapping recipes and cooking tips, while I rocked Jam in his little rocking carrier, with my foot. She asked me about the market garden and baking we had for sale every Saturday. She started laughing, "I always wanted to have a small store, where I could feature my baking and cooking skills. This would be my answer, but who would buy off an old black woman?"

"Other women! Black women because they probably know from your church, that you are an excellent cook. White women because they can see you are a good cook and pretty soon, color won't come into it, as it shouldn't."

We looked at each other. "Don't you have any color bias?" she asked.

"None, do you?"

Then we started laughing all over again, because we both know that sometimes racial bias works both ways, if you are only comfortable around people that are like you. We became fast friends right there and then.

"Tell me about these chicken tractors Marty keeps telling me about."

Mahalia was a college graduate who fell in love with a farmer. She told me she got complacent in her role and let herself get out of shape, and as the children needed her less and less, she got lazy. If she could get a stall up and running, perhaps with a new purpose in life, she would be inspired to look after her health better. She proposed putting her hens to work getting the beds ready for next year.

I walked her kitchen with her, telling her what the Department of Health would be looking at and what they required. She wanted a new sink, so I told her to go to the restaurant supply house in Charlotte and get a stainless-steel triple sink.

"Oh, that's why we have triple sinks at the church. You have to use bleach in the second one and rinse in the third."

"I have to use a dishpan for the third and I get away with it because my mother-in-law's sink, which I inherited, is an heirloom. They like a dishwasher, too, but no way I'll ever have one. Look at the tines of a fork in a restaurant where they serve all-day breakfast and I'll bet you find egg particles stuck there, and that fork went through a commercial dishwasher. That's your argument if they press you. They heard it from me, but I live in another county."

"More than one way to skin a cat," she chuckled. I noticed she had shed her slow backroads speech pattern.

"Usually," I laughed.

Mahalia and Leon visited with us several times that summer, usually on a Monday or Tuesday—our slow days. We shared experiences with them, as they planned to go into the market garden/bakery business the following spring. We promised Leon the use of the seed drill and Ben took it home one Saturday and brought it back the next. We went over there on a Monday, in the fall, and the four of us, plus some of the friends, planted a strawberry field. They had a dog named "Champ" and he was the second best baby-sitter in the world.

# Chapter 27

When Jam could stand on his own two feet, I put him in the first manger on the hay with a toy, while Brian was milking. Jam looked up at the big cow's head above him. She reached down and smelled him. He patted her nose. She ate some hay. They were looking at each other. Jam stood up. The cow put her muzzle closer. Jam put two fingers of one hand up one of her nostrils, "gobblety-gooking" to her all the while. When he withdrew his fingers, I started over before he could put those fingers in his mouth, but the lassie was too quick for me. She swiped his fingers with her prickly tongue; then she gave him a lick up one side of his head and then up the other side. He sat down. She went on eating and he played with his toy.

When I took him out of the manger, his curly, black hair was scrubbed up on both sides into an instant Mohawk hair-do.

"Look, Brian, at his hair. Maybe we should go into interesting hair styles for men and boys," I laughed.

"That kid won't thank you if he's bald when he's eighteen."

"The cow's tongue stimulates his scalp. Anyway, he loves it."

We had supper, then, I bathed Jam. He sat on his dad's knee and we watched baseball for a while, until it was feeding time and off to bed.

The next evening, Jam was in manger number two, and so on down the line. An evening with Elsie, the little Jersey, was the last in the row. He loved the cows.

On Sunday evenings, Brian would play the bagpipes outside the screened porch, while Jam and I sat and enjoyed the glorious sound. Now that Jam could maneuver hanging on to furniture, he bee-lined for the pipes when he saw Brian filling the bag. I thought he might be startled by the sound when he got close, but no, his Scottish instincts kicked in. He put his ear to the bag thinking the sound came from there. When Brian went outside and played, Jam sat on my knee and his foot tapped out the rhythm. A bag-piper-to-be, no doubt.

One morning after breakfast, Brian was bouncing Jam on his knee. Jam had been fussing the day before and had a slight temperature. Examining his mouth, I could see he had two big teeth coming through at once, as his gums were very red.

"Brian, I really wouldn't bounce him like that. He hasn't been feeling well."

"Oh, he's okay, Mom. He's his dad's heir apparent, aren't you, son. Dad's little man. Mommies worry too much. We men have to stick together."

I left them to their play and stepped outside. It was a clear, sunny day. The climbing roses were lovely and smelt so beautiful. I got my clippers and dead-headed the spent blooms.

"Georgie! Georgie! Get in here, pleeeeze!"

I rushed in. "Brian, what's the matter?" He held out the newspaper bundled around the baby. Then the smell hit me.

"Brian, I haven't read that paper yet."

"Well, you won't be reading this one. Here," and he thrust the odiferous clump into my arms. He was sweating profusely and if he wasn't so tanned, I would have said his face would have been a ghastly grey. He rushed outside. As I started for the bathroom, passing by the kitchen windows, I could see him leaning on the table and his sides were heaving.

"Well, little man, let's get you cleaned up. I think you've laid the big man low." Jam giggled.

Shortly after, I took our sweet, bathed and powdered boy out to see his dad.

Brian looked sideways at the baby. Jam smiled a gooey smile at his father

"What the hell was that about?"

"Language, Brian!"

"Sorry. The worst part was he kept chuckling and laughing when the muck was flowing down his legs."

"Of course he was. All that putrefaction has been building up inside of him. Think of the relief he was experiencing. I told you not to bounce him, but I thought he would upchuck his breakfast."

"I'll get you another newspaper," he said sheepishly.

"Don't bother. If there was anything good in it, it will be in the next six issues. If it was bad news, I don't need it. By the way, newspaper dissolves when wet."

"Well, it won't ever happen again." His jaw went clenched.

"Now see here, Brian. You help deliver calves. You put on a long rubber glove and insert your arm up to the shoulder, up the back end of a cow to turn a calf. You clean up after the lassies and sometimes they are not quite done and you get splashed. You swamp out the pigs and scrape out the chicken house. You are no stranger to poop! So get over it."

He stared at me. Jam gurgled. Then suddenly, we were cracking up with laughter. "No stranger to poop," he said. He raised his head and roared.

"Yes, ma'am," he choked out and gave me a mock salute.

I couldn't let him use that incident to get off the hook. Baby-sitting was a shared responsibility. If he went all Scottish and stubborn, I could never go out of sight of the baby. I needed to be free to cruise the woods after a storm looking for windfalls or lightning-shattered trees. I had to be free once I started planting the organic garden in the spring. I had to be free to go shopping and running errands as fast as I could. Why should I be tethered and Jam have his routine disturbed because Daddy was suddenly squeamish? Thankfully, Brian got over it, right then.

He brought out the wicker chairs.

"It's feeding time."

"Why don't you feed him out here. It's so lovely. I'll get your hats."

"Alright,"

While Jam fed, Brian and I held hands. Brian regarded Jam and I with pride.

# Chapter 28

"You know this wee lad's going to need his own lawn chair soon," I remarked one evening.

"Where could we get one?"

"I'm thinking we could make one. I'll go on the internet and see if I can find plans. It would be a great first birthday present."

"See if you can find a pattern."

I did a lot of work on the computer, and I was teaching Brian how to look things up. The record for each cow was kept there and it would have taken a lot of book-keeping to keep up with the records the government needed to see. Every milk inspection and test had to be recorded, as well as daily output of milk, also vaccinations, etc. Our clothes, books, movies, music, tools, and parts for equipment were all ordered electronically.

I scrolled through "Lawn Chairs", "Adult Adirondack Chairs" and "Kid's Plastic Table and Chairs", even though I had specified "Child's Wooden Lawn Chair". Finally, an Australian fellow showed a picture and free instructions.

I printed it out. We looked it over. Brian flashed the tape measure and we decided it was perfect.

The next time Brian went to town, he went to the lumber yard to price the wood. The manager came over and looked at the plans. "Are you making the little table, too?"

"We could."

"Price this out, Bob, and take ten percent off the price. This is the man from whom we buy our logs."

Brian came home with the wood and tickled pink with the price. Scots love a bargain, but then, don't we all?

In our spare time, we built the set. The picture showed it in bright red. We decided to paint it the same way. "We have to be careful to get non-toxic paint suitable for children's furniture." I hadn't thought about that.

Soon, Jam could walk. Brian would put him up on his shoulder and walk the fields with him, looking for disease, weeds, broken fencing and infestations. When he was nearly back to the barn, he set Jam down on his feet. "See the barn. Watch where you are going, but keep going to the barn." Jam trudged along at his own slow pace and Brian followed him. Gradually he could walk further and got stronger as time progressed. Brian started pointing things out to him and what the crops were. "Saw porridge field, Mom"—the oat field. We call oatmeal "porridge". Jam digested information and cut to the chase in reporting what he saw. Brian was using my

Dad's method of teaching us to appreciate the big and the little things we saw on our walks, and then we would have to tell our mom what we had observed. Jam loved to relay what he had seen.

Jam helped me fill the bird feeders. I could accurately pour the seed into the feeders, but I bought him a plastic funnel. He loved it and also used it in his sand box for filling empty plastic bottles or the hoppers on his trucks.

May was a gorgeous month and after a full day of work from before the sun was up until suppertime, we liked to relax on the patio with a lemonade. Jam was sitting on my knee.

"Let's give it to him now." I knew exactly what Brian meant and nodded. He went into the tool shed in the drive shed and came back with the scarlet little lawn chair and table. He set it down. Jam's eyes went big. He loved red.

"There you go, Jam. Look what Mommy and Daddy made just for you."

Jam got down off my knee and slowly approached the chair. Brian put the table to one side. Jam touched each arm, then, very tentatively, put his knees on the seat. Then he swung each leg out to the side and under the arms. There he sat, legs stuck out, facing the back of the chair. We laughed and laughed as Brian lifted him out and turned him around. Brian placed the table in front of the chair. Solemnly, with the visage of an owl, Jam examined table and chair. Suddenly his little face lit up. He patted the arms. "Mine", he declared, triumphantly.

We put his chair between ours and we all used the little table. At night, his table and chair went inside. If we were in the screened porch, there was the little table and chair.

For his second Christmas, I bought him books, toys, slippers and pajamas. His father bought him a plastic (no sharp edges) tape measure and gave him a huge cardboard box. I might have saved my money. He lived in the box in the daytime, and he and Brian measured everything in our lives. He was all male, that boy.

# Chapter 29

Our strawberry business really took off. Marty and Ben had their own farm business to do now, so we had other kids from the Ag. College and we paid them better than minimum wage, as well. They carefully picked the berries and we never had one complaint. We'd had rain earlier, but during the season, the weather was mild but not too hot, and dry.

Our Saturday market had eggs, lettuce, radishes, green onions, and as the season progressed, we added raspberries, blackberries, elderberries, some black sweet cherries (we had to be fast to beat the birds, even though the trees were netted), and later, peppers, tomatoes, cucumbers, cooking onions, herbs, apples and pears. I also put out some baking.

"Isn't that little Adirondack chair and table precious? Where did you ever get it?" young Mrs. McLaren asked. I told her Brian and I made it.

"Golly, do you have any more?"

"Not yet, but we are planning on making more, and of course, we can paint it whatever non-toxic paint color you want. It goes in the house every evening, as our son prefers to sit on it than use his high chair or a kitchen chair."

"How much would you charge?"

"Will you be back next Saturday, Mrs. McLaren?"

"Sure will. I love having access to local produce right from the farm. When I go into the supermarket, everything looks so tired—road fatigue, and the prices! You get the stuff home and in three days there's black mold because everything is encased in plastic and damp. Maybe I only want three carrots, but I have to take a full package and then half gets thrown away. Your produce lasts all week. Your strawberries were the best. I put twelve quarts in the freezer, so we'll be thinking about you people all winter."

"Thank you. What an endorsement. Next week I'll be able to give you a price for the little table and chair."

Later Brian asked, "How will you come up with a fair price?"

"Take the cost of material from the first set, add the ten percent back on the wood because you won't get that bargain again, and double that figure to cover our labor and power costs."

We worked it out and set a fair and firm price.

"Did I hear you dickering on a sale of pies?"

"Yes, I have an order for ten pies, all apple with rum and raisin, for a wedding. Lenore MacAskill is getting married and her husband's family live in Charlotte and are professional people. They've never tasted country cooking. Her mother, grandmother and aunts can do everything but the pies. They bought one last week for a taster and loved it, so they want me to bake the pies."

"How much are you going to charge?"

"It will be ten—ten inch pies cut into seven slices each. They only need about sixty-five slices. I'm charging seven dollars a pie, so seventy dollars for seventy slices and Lenore gave me a twenty dollar deposit."

Brian sat with a smile on his face.

"What?" I asked.

"Would you have ever believed that two shy people like you and I could become customer-friendly?"

"Well, our customers started out few in number and we became friends and that just carried on when the customer numbers swelled."

Yes, things were moving along on the farm. We made plans to double the garden by moving the back fence. The new raspberry bed would soon be in the middle of the garden. Over the fall and winter, the girls would be busy plowing new ground.

"Brian, I think we should extend the dairy to include a full bathroom, with shower, toilet and sink. It's a long run for little legs to run to the house. We have the portable moving wherever the kids are working, but still customers sometimes ask, and I don't like them traipsing through the house while I'm tied up with the cash box."

"I can attest it's a long run for a big boy, too, but let's think about two accesses—one from the dairy and one from the outside. We can lock the dairy door off when the market is open."

Brian sketched it out on paper. "You need room to move around, Brian, if you have a shower and get dressed, so let's make it larger rather than smaller. Also, we need a bigger freezer—could we have room for that?"

"I've been thinking we need a SUV so you can make your deliveries in an enclosed vehicle. I'm nervous when you take the old truck off the farm."

We did have the bathroom built and we did get a SUV, which was good, because we were now getting orders from cafes, delis and restaurants. We had the vehicle painted up with our name and phone number on it so it would qualify as a business expense.

One Wednesday, when I was going on delivery and was packing the back, Brian told me he had bought Jamie a chanter to get him started on the bagpipes eventually. It looked like rain, so that would be a good pastime for the morning.

The next Sunday night, Jamie made a little speech, after he had demonstrated what he had learned to play on the chanter. "Mom, there's a poem about Bonnie Prince Charlie. Now it's a song. Dad's learned for you 'cause you came back to here."

Brian played "Will Ye No Came Back Again?" It was lovely and I cried in appreciation. It was true. I had come back. Thank goodness.

Brian and Jamie came and hugged me. "I told you she 'd cry. Sorry, love."

"You've made me such a softie. Nothing used to touch me. I was tough."

"You've become softer, darling, because you have strong love now. Aye?"

"Aye."

# Chapter 30

"Don't you have a problem with rocks on your farm?" It was Doctor McKay who was asking. He was a dentist in Charlotte, and he and his wife came to our market at least once a month. "My grandparents farmed towards Asheville and the rocks were a curse, especially to mechanized equipment."

"No, not here. In the 20's, a geological team for the government came through this area, and they told my grandfather that this farm was once a tarn—a mountain lake, but something seismic occurred and the river that fed this lake went underground and at the same time, the rocks that formed the southern lip of the lake tumbled down, causing a spillway that drained the lake. If you walk in our woods, you can see the huge boulders that were the lip, tumbled every which way. Wind from the west brought soil and dead vegetation and gradually the lake filled in. My great-grandfather bought this land but he went back to Scotland where he was a barrister. He wanted to retire here but he was made a judge and he never got back, but he inspired his son who came and cleared the farm. Both my father and my grandfather used organic methods of farming because they knew the soil here is precious. We are one hundred percent organic."

On the following Monday, we heard that Gladys Bannister and her boyfriend, Pete Rogers, were killed in a car accident coming home from a weekend at Dollywood. Gladys was Patsy's older sister. They were the only children the Bannisters had. Mick and Patsy flew to Greensboro and rented a car and drove to Patsy's old home. We talked to Mick on the phone.

On Wednesday, we dropped Jamie off at the day care center in Aberfoyle Springs for the day and went to the funeral. We sat with Mom and Dad. It was very sad as there were a lot of children and young people there. Gladys had been the local Girl Scout leader, a Sunday school teacher and she helped with the Young People's Club at the church. She had worked as a receptionist at the Medical Clinic.

The ladies of the church had put out a beautiful buffet and sweets table.

Mr. and Mrs. Bannister sort of button-holed us in the corner and asked us to please try and talk Mick and Patsy in taking over the farm.

"There's an ell on the house where my parents moved to when Iris and I took over the farm. Gladys and Pete were never going to take on the farm. Pete wanted no part of manual labor. He was always trying to find an easier way to make a living. He wanted to chase the fast buck. Gladys had a time with his gambling, I can tell you. I don't think they would ever have got hitched. They'd been engaged for four years," Mr. Bannister told us.

"We can't really influence them. They have to make up their own minds. If they do go for it, and they would be fools not to, we will help them any way we can," Brian assured them.

"I'm not so sure that farm will support four people. It's pretty run-down—lack of money, I suspect." Brian mused as we drove to the day care.

"Five people. Patsy's pregnant."

I paid the day care and Jamie marched rather truculently to the SUV. As I strapped him in, he said," Well, that's the last time I go there."

"Didn't you like playing with the other kids?"

"I liked the toys, but Mom look at my arms," and he held them out. "Those kids all bite." He had several bite marks up his arms.

He was very quiet as we drove along, and we were, too. We were shocked, but more was to come.

"Dad, what do these words mean?" and he fired off a couple of expletives.

I thought Brian was going to run off the road, then, he stopped suddenly. Fortunately, no one was behind us. He put the car in "Park" and turned around to Jamie. "Son, we don't use those kinds of words—not ever. Only stupid people with no intelligence, use those words. You heard those words to-day at day care, didn't you?" Brian asked sternly.

"Yes, sir." His bottom lip was trembling.

"Well, you are right. That is the last time you will ever go there. Mother, I think it's time we looked into homeschooling for Jamie. What do you think?"

"Great idea. I'll look into it and we can start very soon."

# Chapter 31

Mick and Patsy agreed to take over the farm. Since Mick got out of the military, he had been working on a dairy farm in the Hudson Valley of New York state. It was organically farmed and they had a farm dairy. Patsy had been volunteering at a veteran's hospital. Both were able to leave their jobs in two weeks.

When they got moved in, and Patsy's parents had moved to the ell, they invited us to lunch on a Monday. The Bannisters joined us and asked for advice on the direction the farm should take.

The six of us and Jamie walked the property. It was one hundred acres, and I made note of every field—if fallow—for how long, what crop was in it or had been in it, and what fertilizers and pesticides had been used.

They had a nice dairy herd, but it was small. They had Guernseys like ours. They had six chickens and two pigs. They grew blueberries that they sold at a farmer's market but for very little return. I asked them to sell them at our market as long as they hadn't been sprayed. The Bannisters assured me they were clean.

Around the kitchen table, we discussed the farm and opportunities.

"You have to start immediately with a plan for each field, succession crops, and pastureland. Most of your fields already qualify as organic. As the farm sits now, it will not generate enough revenue to sustain four adults and a baby. It takes time to get every field up to snuff. What ideas do you have, Georgie?"

"As you were talking, I was thinking there is no way for this farm but up. Both Mr. and Mrs. Bannister have their health, they are not infirm or aged. Mick has been working on an organic farm with a dairy. Mick helped us out when we were in a corner. Then I got a flash. Remember Steve told us about having a farm dairy, and Mick has just come from a farm dairy. It was too big an undertaking for just Brian and I. Why don't you do that? There's a family farm dairy near Julian, just below Greensboro, and they supply supermarkets, health stores and the market with milk, buttermilk, chocolate milk, butter, cottage cheese, and who knows what else. On the farm, they sell those products plus homemade natural ice cream. Steve said Harris Teeter sells Irish butter from grass-fed cows, all organic and it sells for almost double the price of ordinary butter. If you keep the prices comparable but offer organic, people will come to you, as they do to us. We'll have posters for you and you can display ours. People come from Charlotte to us on a monthly run and that's quite a step. Once here, they want to know what else is available. We have a market for beef, and you could join us in that, pasturing beef cattle."

"That's our Georgie! Her brain is always on overdrive," Brian laughed. The rest looked like deer caught in the headlights. Mick was scribbling like crazy. His creative juices were flowing.

"How much would it cost for start up?"

"I wouldn't know. Our contractor that enlarged our dairy could give you an estimate. We'll give you his name and we can recommend him," shared Brian.

"Gladys had two life insurance policies. One from work and one she took out when she was eighteen. I am the beneficiary on both. They are small but do you think twenty thousand would get us started?" asked Patsy.

"Why wasn't Pete the beneficiary?" asked Mrs. Bannister.

"If they got married, she would have changed it to Pete, but she told me I was to have it. Gladys had a heart murmur and that bothered her. I think somehow she knew she might die young." Patsy mopped her eyes.

We left shortly after, but Mick and Brian had a private chat before we drove away.

On the way home, he told me Mick also had some money put away from when he was overseas that he hadn't touched yet, and Mom and Dad told them they would give them a hand up, as well.

"They'll be fine. Mrs. Bannister is one of the marvelous cooks from the church, and did you see her eyes light up at the thought of a dairy. With a Health Department certificate on the dairy, she can bake there and sell her products."

We went home and after milking and supper, it was reading night. Jamie loved this night because he had his own shelf of books We took turns reading his book to him, listening to him repeat the story, then, we all go to our own books. We'd help him with another of his, and proceed the same way until his bed time. We all loved "Reading Night".

# Chapter 32

One day, when Jamie was four, I was standing at the end of the hall looking out at the garden.

"What are you looking at, sweetheart?"

"Do you think we could add onto the house on this side?"

A few minutes passed.

He turned me around and looked into my eyes. "Are we pregnant?"

"I'm feeling broody and I think I might be. I'm going to get a test to-day."

He turned me back around to face the window, laughing all the time. "Are you thinking of two rooms? A nursery and a spare room?"

"That's what I'm thinking."

"And how did this happen, Georgie?"

"I beg your pardon?"

"Well, we've always taken precautions, so how could this happen?"

"Will you stop talking as if you weren't there at the conception. I do remember a couple of times over the years when we were unprepared and someone couldn't wait. Do you remember this past July fourth? Setting off a few firecrackers for Jamie, and we had sparklers and a couple of wine spritzers. Someone didn't want to wait then."

"We were celebrating, and anyway, I was just fooling around."

"And God said 'Go forth and multiply' and Man thinks he so smart what with the rhythm method, birth control pills, condoms, and so on, and 'just fooling around', to get around His command, so when Man gets caught, God must laugh. I bet He's saying 'Gotcha, Brian' right now."

"You think you know what God is thinking, don't you?"

"If you think God doesn't have a sense of humor, I can give you lots of examples that He does."

"I'll take your word for it. I'll get the contractor back to give us an estimate, and Georgie, think about this. You need help. Put up a notice and see if anyone applies. Don't you think an expansion will encroach on the garden?"

"It's thirty-two feet to the garden from the house wall. The extension should be sixteen feet. That leaves sixteen feet to the fence. Ample room for the contractor to work."

"Of course, you have measured it?"

"Of course."

"What if it's another boy? Jamie could share."

"No, he can't. That's his space, with his belongings. We want him to love this little brother, if that's what we have, not resent him from Day One. Every child should have their own room of dreams, if possible."

# Chapter 33

Construction started right away. We kept out of the way, as we were busy with our own projects.

We had bought a child's computer desk and we put it in the kitchen between the window and the entry door. We got a little swivel chair and a computer for Jamie and signed him up for home schooling. He could already count to one hundred, knew his alphabet, colors and could tell time—which turned him into a little nag for a while, for if we were late doing something, Jamie would be there, tapping his watch-face. He took a test to determine where he should start his education, and he was to start at Grade one. Not bad for a four and a half year old.

We were selling our "Child's Lawn Chair and Table" as fast as we could make them although we only displayed them one at a time. Brian's hand was determined to be ninety-five percent recovered and only the cold sensitiveness was the obstacle to one hundred percent. The therapist said that would fade with time.

I was getting orders for baking every week now. People knew they had to order by Wednesday to pick up the goods on Saturday morning. I displayed our health certificate in a weather-proof picture frame near the baking stall. When the weather was inclement, Brian cleared out the drive shed and we moved in there.

I posted a notice for "Help Wanted" along with a menu of baking for sale—cookies, squares, butter tarts, muffins, fruitcake, fruit and nut loaves, tea cakes and pies.

Gran sent me her mother's recipe for a special smoked sausage popular in England at the turn of the century, called Cumberland Sausage. We went to our butcher, Mr. Ramsay, and he sold us pig intestines, cleaned, brined and ready to be used as casings for the sausages. We bought a smoker. Brian's mom had a big meat grinder, complete with sausage stuffer. We made up the mixture, stuffed it, and Brian smoked them in the backyard. Mr. Ramsay gave us some recipes for bratwurst and kielbasa, he had meant to try. We invited him and his son, Jack, to supper the first time we tried the Cumberland, served with steamed cabbage, applesauce and mashed potatoes. Dessert was raspberry cream pie.

"Brian, I'll take all you want to put in the butcher shop on consignment."

They came to a financial agreement, and we would also sell at our market. We didn't tell Mr. Ramsay, but Mick and Patsy were just about to go into raising organic pigs.

We had Mick, Patsy, Iris and Brandon Bannister over for lunch and gave them samples of all three sausages for their lunch along with coleslaw and scalloped potatoes. After the men went outside to look at the pigs, I showed Patsy and Iris our baking menu, and then the computer work necessary to satisfy the government and its departments.

"I thought I was going to take a job off the farm, but what with computer records, health aspects of family, animals and farm, the baby and the dairy, I'm going to be too busy to go out to work. Hurrah!"

Later Brian said to me, "Besides hiring help, perhaps you need more modern equipment."

"No. when it's hot, I can bake at night, anyway we'll slow down in November."

"I only meant there is room in the pantry for an electric stove, and the air conditioner can cope to reduce the heat. That's a big furnace and A/C with huge capacity." So Brian and I bought a large electric stove.

That Saturday, Ruby Montgomery (the lady who sniffed all the time), said, "What all is required of the help you are looking for? And how much does it pay?"

"Washing dishes, scrubbing pans, chopping vegetables, peeling things, helping mix the sausage mixtures. Whatever comes up in the seven hours. We pay two dollars an hour over the minimum wage and lunch is provided."

"Myrtle, you can do that. She can iron and launder, too."

"Oh, we don't own anything that requires ironing."

"That so?" and she looked me up and down and gave a loud sniff. Ruby was a person very full of herself. Nothing passed at the church Ladies' Gathering without her approval. She was a take charge type of person—certainly an "A" personality. You felt you needed to tiptoe when she was around, to avoid being centered out.

Myrtle, we knew from church, and she was slow, shy and very quiet. I took her through to the screened porch. She was very slim and tall in a faded cotton dress and her hair up in a net.

"Are you sure you want this job, Myrtle?"

"Yes, Mrs. MacKenzie. It would be wonderful to be away from Ruby all day long. I'm the poor relation and she never lets me forget it. This way I can hand over my paycheck and feel I'm contributing. I'd love to work here again. You haven't changed a thing. I used to work for Miz Janet when I was younger. I imagine everything is where it once was."

"You can probably teach me how you and Janet did things. Would you like to start on Monday? I'll pick you up. I'm Georgie."

"No, Everett can bring me for nine and pick me up. Thank you, Georgie."

# Chapter 34

Myrtle was a treasure and she was not slow. She was afraid of Brian at first.

She had never seen him before because he was always working. Each week I posted a list of the kitchen activities. She and I knew every day who was doing what. We put time frames on every activity.

"Myrtle, you probably noticed I have a bump. I'm going to have a baby next April, so I have to be careful not to overwork you when I get real heavy and clumsy. You let me know. Now would you like to see the hens plowing?"

She looked at me funny, but when she saw the girls in action, she laughed with delight.

"Myrtle, I'm going to work in my greenhouse. Would you like to see it?"

She followed me to the basement with a curious look on her face. She looked at everything. I was really just cleaning as most of the season was over, but soon in January, we would be in full swing again.

"Mrs . . . . Georgie, this is amazing."

She loved Jamie, who called her "Mertie", even though we told him repeatedly she was Miss Sinclair. "Could you all call me Mertie? It's what my Dad called me. Myrtle is such a brittle name."

When Mertie was chopping fruit or vegetables or soaking raisins, she always saved a piece for Jamie and when he finished his lessons, he knew a tidbit would be waiting for him. She loved Buster too, and kept a little meat trimming for him. Both boy and dog adored her. We worked together well, never getting in each other's way. She peeled the apples. I made the pastry. We put them together assembly line fashion. When Jamie was finished for the day, he selected a CD of classical music for us to listen to while he went out to see if his dad had a chore put aside for him.

One afternoon, Mertie stopped still. "What was that wonderful piece of music?"

"It's from Vivaldi's Four Seasons. That was 'Spring' don't you love it?"

She did and she was developing a real "ear" for the classics.

"Do you like the bagpipes?"

"Oh, yes. Ruby's father-in-law played records of bagpipe bands. I love it."

"Brian plays the pipes. He plays for us every Sunday night."

# Chapter 35

One day in January, Mertie came to work very down in the dumps, and Everett spun his wheels when he left.

She wouldn't say what the matter was. An hour later, the paring knife slipped and she cut her finger. I cleaned the little cut, but suddenly she started to sob, and put her apron over her face.

I put my arms around her. She leaned into me. I held her until she calmed.

"I'm going to make us a pot of tea."

"Oh, Georgie, we'll be behind in the schedule."

"Hang the schedule! You are more important than chopped vegetables." I put the cups down. "What is it, Mertie?"

"Everett and Ruby put their house up for sale and didn't tell me. Now they have sold it and bought a condo in Florida. There's no room for me. I'm to go in that assisted living place where you go if you have no money. Ruby says this job will soon peter out."

"Oh, Mertie. You're too active and useful to go and vegetate."

She cried more.

"My dear Mertie, I want you to cheer up and take it to the Lord. Things will turn out. Have faith. I believe that. Have a good long chat with God to-night."

"Will that help?"

"You'll see. It can't hurt."

In bed that night, I told Brian what was happening.

"I'm surprised they kept her as long as they did. People say they were working her to death. Not nice people—the Montgomerys. Myrtle hasn't lived with them long. She lived with her mother in that little white house by the library. Her mother drove her here and was a good friend of my mother's. They both spoke Gaelic, as Mrs. Sinclair was a McIsaac right out from Scotland."

"What can we do, Brian?"

"Let's think about it. Have a pray about it, Georgie."

In the morning, she crept in and was very quiet.

"So did you tell God about your situation?"

"I think He was busy."

"No. He wasn't. There's an answer. He'll give it to you and it won't be anything any of us would have thought of."

Brian came in for mid-morning tea and Mertie scuttled away.

"Mertie, can you come back here, please. I need to talk to you."

She sidled into her chair.

"Do you have any other relatives, Mertie?"

"No."

"Good."

I looked at him. "Sweetheart, you like working with Mertie and she is going to be a great help to you as you get closer to having this baby."

"Absolutely! We thought the baking would end in November, but we were swamped for Christmas and now all these shops want 'natural' baking. Mertie is so necessary, besides we get along so well."

"Mertie, you love Jamie, we can tell. Can you get used to me? I'm big but I'm harmless."

"I know, Mr. MacKenzie, and I love all of you."

"From now on, it's Brian. Georgie is going for a scan today to make sure everything is fine with the baby. She has negative blood so they have to monitor her. I have an idea in mind, but I have to talk it over with her. Keep up with those prayers, both of you." We nodded.

We came home in shock. Twins! A boy and a girl! We talked into the night. Our solution was to move Mertie into the spare room, but this changed our plans.

The next morning, Everett dropped off a completely dejected Mertie. He continued to the barn to talk to Brian. After he left, I went to the barn.

"What's up?"

"What a pompous oaf. They are leaving to-morrow and to-day is Mertie's last day. She goes to the poor house to-night."

"It's not a poor house."

"Might as well be for a person like Mertie. It'll be like a prison to her."

"Well, we can't do what we were going to do."

"No, but maybe we can do something else."

# Chapter 36

Later that morning, Brian buzzed passed the house, his magic tape measure in his hand. What was he doing? He came in.

"Any tea going?"

I put out three cups of tea, and milk for Jamie, who was doing lessons on the computer. Mertie brought the milk jug and the stevia (sugar substitute).

"Mertie, you are like an auntie to us. Jamie, you better hear this too. Georgie is going to have twins. I want to take you to Ruby's and I'll wait while you pack up your belongings."

"Everything is packed."

"Good. We'll bring your things here. The spare room is yours for now, but we, the four of us, are going to have a room and bathroom built to the right of the kitchen. That window between the china cabinet and Jamie's desk will be your door. What do you all think?"

The apron went up over her face. Laughing, Brian got up and hugged her.

"Mertie's going to live with us? Hurray. But twins—that's two babies."

"Yes, Jamie. Two babies—one of each. A brother and a sister!"

"I love this family so much. I thought I would never see you again. That's what I couldn't bear."

"You see. We all prayed and we couldn't have imagined what the Lord would come up with, could we?" I hugged her.

"Really, I have no idea where the idea came from. It just sort of hit me, so I guess you were right, Georgie, 'my help cometh from the Lord'."

Brian drove Mertie to the Montgomery's and brought her back with her meager things. Then she and I went to town in the truck and bought a double bed, dresser, and vanity table with ornate stool. We bought bed linen, a bedspread, pillows, towels and toiletries. We were like school girls let loose. We had fun. She objected at first and looked at cheap furniture, but I steered her to the quality furnishings.

The spare bedroom was painted dusty rose with a rose border with the roses spilling over the edges. There were white Priscilla curtains and a double blind. The room was unfurnished until we got home.

Brian and I set up the bed. I put the new linen in the washer. Brian and Mertie positioned the dresser and vanity. We left her to unpack.

"You know we think the world of her. No way would we let the Montgomerys put her out on the curb like last week's garbage," Brian fumed.

We had been told Mertie was slow, but she wasn't at all. She had been down-trodden all her life. Her mother had been overbearing like Ruby. Apparently, her father, who worked at the bank, was a quiet, shy man. He and Mertie were close, both shoved aside as not important.

The Montgomerys moved away and I can't say the community missed them. The ladies of the church, who never talked out of turn, seem relieved to be beyond the beck and call, Alex told us.

The next week, when I gave Mertie her pay, she didn't want to take it.

"Nonsense. You earned it."

"But what would I do with it?"

"Let's go to town, to the bank and you can open an account."

"This is where my father worked," she said, as we approached the service desk. We sat down and the lady there passed an application for an account to Ruby, then she went off to get a number, pass book and checkbook.

"Miss Sinclair, you already have a savings account."

"I do?"

"Yes, but there hasn't been any movement for eight years and in two more years, it will disappear, absorbed into the banking system. Notices were sent out, but never answered."

Mertie deposited her money. "Look how much money is in the account, Georgie." Apparently Mr. Sinclair had opened the account for Mertie and deposited money each month in it for years, until he died.

"Mertie, you are a woman of means."

Brian was so pleased for her. "Your father loved you."

"Yes, he did. I have to tell you, I don't want you to pay me anymore."

"I was thinking about that, and I knew you wouldn't want a wage. You are no longer staff. You are family. Everything on this farm makes money. The money from the lumber company goes to Brian as part of his legacy. Same with the milk money. The egg money is mine. The pork and beef money we divide.

Now the profit from the sausage business, which is a real money-maker, will be shared by the three of us. The market stall and all baking profits will be shared by you and me. Mertie if you will give us a hand with the little chairs and tables, we will split the profits on that. How does that suit everybody?" We all agreed. Mertie was over the moon.

"Mertie, we have evening happenings every evening. I play the spinet and we all sing; one evening we dance; we listen to country-western music one evening; we have reading night; game night; and sports night. Sunday night, Brian plays the bagpipes for us. We eat our suppers outside or in the screened porch as much as we can. We want you to join us in everything we do. Oh, on Sundays, we go to church, as I know you do, and Alex comes for Sunday supper."

"Mom, can we name my baby brother 'Charlie'? You know like Bonnie Prince Charlie?"

"What a great idea, Jamie. That's a good name. He won't be Charles, just Charlie—no second name—just the princely name of Charlie."

"I was trying to think of a good name for the boy and that's perfect, but I was thinking the baby girl should be named after her grandmothers. How about Bess Janet? Nana's name is 'Bess'—not Elizabeth. My Mom was Janet."

# Chapter 37

By the end of January, construction had started on Mertie's quarters. Orders for baking had slowed down, but we were still busy. The seed catalogues had arrived over Christmas, and now the three of us were reading them, making notes as we went. The expanded garden would allow us to experiment with a few new things. We planned a raised bed of all Oriental vegetables for stir-fries, both for us and our café customers. Lots of herbs! We ordered two elderberry bushes for the new corners as Brian loved elderberry pie. We did harvest them from along the fence lines, but you had to be very quick to beat the birds to wild elderberries. We planned to grow ours in netted cages. Our orders went in and by the first of February, our seeds were on hand. By the third week of February, we planted the English peas, as they love the cold. We planted a few sweet peas at the end of the rows for decoration.

Brian and I were still making the little chair and table sets and we sold them unassembled, but painted, over the internet. Mertie helped with the painting. We could sell them as fast as we made them, they were that popular.

All four of us worked in the greenhouse in the afternoon. We were growing some flowers to sell this year as potted plants—geraniums, salvias, verbenas, petunias, coleus, lamium (dead nettle) and an ornamental biennial mullein called "Banana Custard". Each section of plants had a marker with the plant name, date planted, date to set out, and the conditions the plant would need—such as full sun, good in dry area or water requirements, and the eventual height and width. We now had three long workbenches actively involved, each with its own florescent light on adjustable chains. As we thinned the seedlings, we kept the greens for the hens.

Mick and Patsy had made a commitment with the government and entered into a reforestation program to plant trees of the government's choices along the western side of the farm to reduce soil erosion. The same construction company we had, were finishing the dairy construction there. Dairy machinery had been ordered and the Health Department was working with them to make sure things were up to snuff right from the get-go. Patsy and Iris had the décor all worked out and were ready to go as soon as the crew left and the walls were dried enough.

Alex came to us for Sunday night supper. We had moved our big meal to an evening meal to give Alex and us more time to prepare after church. Brian and I sat on the periwinkle pew. We had some merry times.

Mertie like me was not a big eater and she loved the Mediterranean Diet.

During the week, we would put out a platter of chopped vegetables, dried figs or prunes, cheese, pineapple chunks and olives with a lemon or lime vinaigrette. We didn't drink with our meal to maximize the stomach juices for better digestion. A light dessert would follow. We ate fish three to four times a week. Meat was for Sunday. We ate quinoa, brown rice, and oatmeal breading. One slice of artisan bread each, with either virgin olive oil and toasted, or a little butter (homemade, of course).

For breakfast, we might have our own steel-cut oatmeal, with vegan powder, chia seeds, chopped pecans, stevia, raisins, dried cranberries or blueberries. Brian's favorite was our own Canadian-style bacon with eggs, whole wheat brown bread and homemade sweet red pepper relish.

Lunch could be an open-faced sandwich with fruit. Soup in winter. We drank lots of fresh spring water, tea, green tea, milk and occasionally a small glass of North Carolina Duplon wine diluted with gingerale. Special occasions were still celebrated with a glass of wine, or those wine spritzers, we like so incautiously.

When Mertie's room and bath were done, she was delighted and chose the same décor as the spare room. We bought her a small television set as a house-warming gift and

Brian was able to splice it into our satellite line. Alex gave her two framed lithographed pictures of a male and a female hummingbird painted by a well-known wildlife artist, as hummingbirds were her passion.

We redecorated the "spare room" in pink with white and pale green trims. The boy's room, we made pale blue with navy and yellow trims.

Mertie and I loved to walk through the garden, after we set Jamie up with his lessons. We selected food for supper and made note of any jobs that were required. The garden combined with the pantry fare, the basement jars and the freezers gave us inspiration for every meal and our baking.

Mertie and I and sometimes Brian, had canned, pickled and froze everything we could. We even had bags of beef and chicken stock ice cubes in the freezer. As fruits progressed this year, we planned to make small tubs of ice cream for year round treats.

"What are you girls doing to-day?" Brian asked as he came in for lunch one day. "We're making yoghurt and cottage cheese." He just grinned and shook his head. Mertie and I were always trying new things. Most worked; some didn't, but then that's what dogs are for.

# Chapter 38

One Sunday, Alex shared with us that he was planning to retire after Christmas. We were dismayed, but he said, "No. Now is the time. There's a young Presbyterian man in Mocksville who's about to be ordained. A terrific young man. I know his parents well. They came from Scotland in 1986. His name is Dougal McFeeters. He has one more course he wants to take and that ends in December. Now, my youngest sister, Elsbeth, in Scotland, just lost her husband, Jock, last year. Jock was an alcoholic for the past thirty odd years. He was a car salesman in a large dealership that belonged to his cousin. I think that's how he held his job. His drinking started after soccer matches—you know—out with the lads, and then it progressed to an everyday part of his life. They had no children, luckily. Elsbeth stood by him even though she is teetotal. Elsbeth is the only cook in a well-known restaurant in Perth. She worked there all her life for the same people, but they got old and have just sold the business to a young Greek. The new owner keeps saying he needs a real chef and asking does she do 'moussaka' and why don't they stock 'ouzo'. She says he might as well be speaking Greek, which of course, he is—her little joke. Anyway, the writing was on the wall, so she is quitting. Our only other sibling is the eldest and she's in a nursing home in Glasgow. She loves it there. She paints, plays bridge and is quite at home. Elsbeth says she could never stand the 'cloistered life'. I've asked her to come and live with me. She might like small town country living. So she's coming in three weeks. As you know, I own my little house and Leila O'Halloran comes in to clean and do laundry. I eat all my meals at the Bluebird Café. I'm hopeful this change will suit us both. I can't see Elsbeth eating every meal at the Bluebird where everything, including breakfast, tastes Chinese."

"Oh, Alex, are you sure you won't be bored?"

"Never. There's so many books I never had time to read. Old movies I never saw, plus I want to show Elsbeth some of this country. We can go to the mountains, the beach, Washington, D.C. when the cherry blossoms are out. We'll just play it by ear. I'm hopeful we'll get along fine. We are the closest in age and were always grand pals. I think we need each other at this stage of our lives."

We were happy for him if he was happy and we looked forward to welcoming his sister.

The next week, he was not so happy. We had just come through a couple of days of nasty rainstorms. "Brian, a long stretch of guttering came down. I got your contractor, Fred

Cooper, to look at it. He tacked it up temporarily, but said all the guttering is shot. It's rusted, twisted and the supports are all gone. He gave me two estimates. One is to replace the whole thing and the second is the same, only to finish it off with 'leaf guards' that apparently stop leaves from building up, causing blockages which force the water up on the roof. Both are staggering amounts. What can we do? Any suggestions?"

"I'd take it to the Lord, and the congregation. Put out a big jar for donations. We'll give you a big pickle jar and a donation. Time is of the essence because the fall rains will come soon enough."

"You know the tithes just cover the bills and maintenance. I've declined an increase for the last six years, and that's okay, because I'm preaching on borrowed time and felt it was a privilege. For any extra project in the past, the ladies, the backbone of any organization, rolled up the sleeves and fund raised."

Two weeks later, Alex brought Elsbeth to supper. We had met her at church and looked forward to getting to know her better. She was more than middle age and a very bubbly person. Her smile lifted you up and her humor kept you aloft. We had a hilarious supper with anecdotes from both sides of the "pond", as Elsbeth put it.

"How's the fund-raising coming along?" asked Brian.

# Chapter 39

Alex soberly replied, "Not so well. In fact, not well at all. There's your check for five hundred and then twenty-two dollars, all in ones, and that's it."

"We'd better call for a congregational meeting," Brian stated. "We need to seriously raise money and quickly. There's less than six months until the heavy rains start."

"The church ladies wondered if a big bake sale would help." Mertie passed along. "They are prepared to make meat pies, cabbage rolls and meat sticks in large quantities. They'll have an 'all hands on deck' cooking day at the church. As you know, we have a Board of Health certificate that says we can cook for the public from the church kitchen."

"Alex, why don't we ask them to hold their bake sale here on a Saturday in May—say the second Saturday. The strawberries will be ready and we will have a huge crowd. I could add it to our ads in the papers as a special attraction. Mertie, what do you think, could we donate our profit from that day to the fund-raiser."

"Sure we could."

"How about the profit from the sausage sales for that day?" asked Brian.

"Oh, that's wonderful but we can't let you do it all, "Alex exclaimed.

"We'll have the meeting after church this Sunday, and tell them what you are prepared to do and what the ladies will do, and see what happens."

"Alex, the nursing home and the senior apartment complex each have buses. Do you think these establishments would transport our seniors to church next Sunday?" I asked.

"Could we have a sandwich, tea and some dessert after church just before the meeting?" practical Mertie wanted to know.

"I'll contact the management of the seniors' different residences and make that request, after all, those residents have been the movers and shakers in the past. I'll ask Dorcas Findlay to ask her ladies to provide sandwiches and I'll donate donuts. Our beloved North Carolina donut company sent a letter advising they can supply donut varieties at a reduced price for any event."

"You know Alex, I was thinking of the skills those ladies in the senior places have, that is no longer used. For example, Bertie MacPherson is an artist. Does she still paint? Helen Crawford made beautiful cloth pocketbooks. Cleo McIntee is a full-blooded Cherokee and a wonderful basket weaver, making wicker baskets, picnic baskets and wastepaper baskets. All these ladies think their skills are not wanted. Their families have enough of their crafts in their homes and don't want anymore, but will the public want those items? I think so."

"Whoa now, Georgie.! Don't get carried away. Your due date is this next week and you are having twins. Your time for organizing will be limited. Keep your ideas coming, but don't plan on visiting these ladies or anything like that."

"I'll keep a lid on her, Brian," laughed Mertie, "or try to and won't you help me, Jamie?" I childishly stuck out my tongue at the three of them.

"You know, Alex, this is upsetting and stressful for you. I wonder if you shouldn't ask young Mr. McFeeters to come to the meeting? He needs to know what he's inheriting. It's not tea and scones with the ladies all the time."

"You're right, Brian. People do have the ridiculous notion that a pastor only works one hour a week."

Elsbeth wondered, "What does the Board of Managers think?"

"They are devastated and overwhelmed at the amount needed to do the replacement. We can't be too harsh with them as they are all over seventy."

# Chapter 40

The meeting was held April 8ᵗʰ and was well attended. Each bus from the seniors' residences made several trips transporting our seniors to church. The lunch was appreciated then, we cleared the tables and went back into the sanctuary where there was a table up front for the pastor, Board of Managers, Mertie, Brian and I. Jamie sat in the front pew near Mertie. Miss Bain, our church secretary, sat at a small table to the side. Miss Bain had been my First Grade teacher.

Some of the suggestions would involve more work and preparation than the small amount of money it would raise, but Miss Bain recorded every idea. Then Elsbeth put up her hand.

Alex recognized the speaker, "For those that might not know, this is Elsbeth Brown, my sister and the newest resident and member of the congregation. Elsbeth, you have the floor."

"Excuse ma accent and perhaps I should just be an observer, but I'd like to share a similar situation we had in Scotland. Three years ago, in Perth, we had tae raise monaes fer a new roof for the kirk—that's church. We ladies put on a sit-doon chicken dinner complete wi' dinner rolls, potatoes, coleslaw, and poodin' fer afters. It's nae sa mooch werk. We charged the equivalent a' ten dollars fer adults and five fer under six. A wee bit more that a meal at McDonald's. We served one hundred and thirteen people—that's ninety adults and twenty-three children, which raised one thousand and fifteen dollars. I know exactly, because I was the cook. Our expenses were fer charcoal, butter, sour cream, mayonnaise, milk, rolls, sugar, tea and juice, paper plates and plastic utensils, napkins and garbage bags-less than one hundred and fifty dollars. The chicken, potatoes, cabbages and carrots were all donated. What do you think? Is it doable?"

Everyone sat stunned by the enormity of the undertaking. "Who would make the desserts?" asked one elderly gentleman.

"Mertie and I can make the pies—apple, rum and raisin, is our most popular pie. We make ten a week now. We'd only need twenty pies—we cut the ten inch pies into seven slices. We'll donate the pies."

"We'll donate the ice cream and take care of serving it on the pie," said Mick, and Patsy nodded.

"Who's got a big enough barbecue?"

"Nae, nae," Elsbeth protested. "Ye make a long dirt base and burn some wood on it. When ye are ready, start up the brickets. Have on hand, metal frames.

Put the frames along the length of the base. You can lift up a section to put more charcoal on. Put sections of steel mesh on top, swab it wi' oil and barbecue on the mesh, moppin' wi' sauce as it cooks. Make the sauce sweet and sour, not spicy— suits everyone. Oh, and by-the-by, sell the tickets in advance."

"Who could bake the potatoes?"

"Ye can. Men will come to yer door wi' a Styrofoam cooler o' foil-wrapped potatoes. Load both racks of the oven. Bake at three hundred and fifty for one hour and fifteen minutes. Put a bowl of hot water in the cooler, put the lid on. When the tatties—sorry—potatoes are fork tender, take the water out of the cooler. Stack in the potatoes and put the lid on. The men will be there shortly and take away yer cooler that's now a heater."

A long silence followed.

"Ye could do what we did and hold an auction of donated new items and raise even more monae."

Brian leaped to his feet, "Thank you, Elsbeth. I think we should really try to do this." Cheers and clapping broke out, even a whistle.

Helen Crawford waved her hands. "Yes, Helen?" asked Alex.

"We ladies and gents from the senior apartments all have stoves we hardly ever use as we have toaster ovens. We could bake the potatoes. You'd only have one place to deliver and pick up." More cheers and old Mr. Bailey waved his cane and shouted, "We're not useless, you know." Mr. Bailey at ninety-two, is usually a very dear and quiet man who used to be our rural mailman.

Mertie held up her hand. All these shy people, including Brian and I, suddenly inspired to speak. "I'd like us to hold a big ceilidh, like we used to have, only have it in the school auditorium. The young people would love it because they can dance with anyone—young or old, and they'd be learning the old dances and keeping them alive. Perhaps in September?"

"Now, I must bring it to your attention that the Mackenzies and Mertie have invited our ladies to hold their bake sale on the second Saturday of May at MacKenzie's because their strawberries will be in full swing and they get huge crowds at that time. Our ladies will also have meat pies, cabbage rolls and meat sticks, so stock up your freezers. Georgie and Mertie will donate their profit from their baking to the building fund, as well Brian will donate the profits from the sausage sales for that day. Georgie reminded us that a lot of our seniors in residences have wonderful skills which they may want to use to enhance the big Saturday sale. Mrs. MacPherson, you might like to sell some paintings, and perhaps donate a portion of your takings. Mrs. McIntee, do you still weave your beautiful baskets? Mrs. Crawford, have any cloth pocketbooks? Think what you can contribute—move your crafts and donate a portion. There will be no charge for a table, and Brian says all will be indoors in the big drive shed if it rains.

Miss Bain was scribbling frantically.

Suddenly, I put my hand on Brian's arm. Everyone was talking at once. Ideas were sparking around the room.

"Brian."

"Just a minute, sweetheart, I want to hear what Ted is saying."

"BRIAN!" I shrieked, as the pain hit me. The room went silent. "The babies are coming."

He jumped to his feet, dug out his keys and threw them to Mertie.

"Mertie, open the car doors. Jamie go with Mertie." He turned and scooped me up in his arms. I threw my arms around his neck, closed my eyes and buried my face in his neck. He strode down the center aisle.

"Everyone was sidling along the pews away from the center aisle. It was like the parting of the Red Sea," Alex told us later.

# Chapter 41

Mertie had all the doors open. Brian gently set me down in the front passenger seat and put on the seat belt. Mertie handed him the keys, and she scrambled into the back seat with Jamie. I heard the doors close and two seat belts snapped into place. Brian ran around the nose, leaped in the car, slammed the door closed, and took off, squealing the wheels. He drove like a madman through town to the hospital, without his seat belt on!

The twins were born and cleaned up forty minutes later.

"Now that was a speedy delivery," exclaimed Doctor McCutcheon, "they were fighting to get out. Easy as passing two grapes."

"Two grapes! Obviously, Doctor, you have never given birth!"

"Perhaps I did exaggerate. Sorry, Georgia."

"Can Mertie and Jamie come in now?"

"Sure they can. The babies are ready." The nurse handed him both and went to call Mertie and Jamie. The doctor held the babies down for Jamie to see.

"Wow, are they ugly! They look like the trolls in Billy Goat Gruff, only red. Will they get better looking?" We all laughed.

"You did, Jamie. You looked just like that," and he passed the bundles to Brian and I.

"That's funny. A newborn baby calf looks like a calf when it's born, and a baby pig looks like a baby pig. I thought these guys would look like real babies."

"When you see them next, they will look like real babies. You'll see."

"When can I go home?" I asked.

"I bet you think you are ready now, but I want you to rest for twenty-four hours. I know you are a type A personality, but this time is best for you. Shall we say after lunch to-morrow afternoon. I will give you a suggestion sheet for coping with twins. You will be lacking sleep for at least six weeks until you can get to the point where they are both sleeping through the night."

When we got them home, we found they were very different than Jamie had been. They were quieter and as long as they were bundled side by side, they seemed very content.

"Which is my brother and which is my sister?"

I had been using white receiving blankets, but changed to pink and blue. Jamie liked to sing to them after they were fed, but was disappointed that they drifted off to sleep every time.

I bought a breast pump, as recommended, and pumped off some milk every feeding. When I had a bottle ahead, someone else could feed one baby. It is very draining feeding two babies at once, and that's no joke. The brochure recommended that if one baby awoke and wanted fed, wake the other one and feed it too. It takes about forty-five minutes to feed one baby. When you finish, that baby will want to be fed again in about two hours. Now, guaranteed, the other baby now wants fed—another forty-five minutes. You will have one hour and fifteen minutes before you start the process again. Feed them together and you will have about two hours free time before you start nursing again. As the baby adjusts to the quality of the milk and becomes more adept at nursing, the nursing time will reduce. I found after two weeks, they were sleeping longer that two hours and that was a blessing to all of us.

"They are just more content. We may have to call you 'Jersey' instead of Georgie," joked Brian.

"You eat a lot of vegetables, organic meat and drink our lovely milk, so it would figure that your milk would be better quality than someone who didn't eat properly, so I can see them being more content," reasoned Mertie.

Patsy and Mick, whose son, Nicholas, was a sturdy little boy and could stay with his grandparents, came over on Saturday mornings, to help Mertie and Brian on the stall. Patsy brought baking by her and her mother to sell. We displayed and orally promoted their all-natural dairy with that lovely natural ice cream—B&M Home Dairy. Iris and Brandon manned the dairy on Saturday mornings.

# Chapter 42

By the end of April, we were back up to full production. We hired Leila O'Halloran to clean on Mondays, just to keep us up to snuff. Each week, Mertie and I made five extra apple pies and froze them unbaked. These were for the big dinner when it happened. Our two Ag girls were busy mulching the vegetable garden, watering plants and helping in the greenhouse by bringing up plants. They checked on the steers, and checked fencing. They picked strawberries and kept the straw mulch in place. They moved the dog/chicken pen as needed.

"The place I was at last year," Valerie told me, "all I did was weed. The whole summer. Other than learning to identify weeds, that's all I learned. I love it here, there is so much going on."

"You are too valuable to us to use you that way. Anyway, the chickens do a better job as they can complete the whole operation from weeding to cultivating and fertilizing. We hope we are giving you much more scope. Tell us if you want to try or see something in production. At lunch, you are giving us new ideas and facts all the time. So it works both ways."

"We are both doing a paper on the effects of no-till and organic methods of farming which we probably wouldn't see except on a government-run farm. To grab a handful of soil in your fields tells the whole story. The rotting winter cover crop is alive with worms who aerate the soil and whose castings enrich it while the vegetation reduces soil erosion, so that even if the summer is dry, the topsoil is not only in place but growing, and thirdly eating up greenhouse gases. We brought our cameras and took pictures to enhance the papers we are going to turn in as proof that organic farming using no-till and cover crop procedures work like nature intended. Megan and I are in different years, so we are not competing against each other. We hope the college will contact you to see if they can bring students out to see firsthand how this farm works."

"We can't take the credit. Brian's dad and grandfather realized what a precious plot of land they had and never used fertilizers or pesticides, so we had no trouble getting this farm certified." Then I told them about the beliefs of the geologists that this was once a mountain lake. They were fascinated. These girls were very keen and loved the soil. I recognized myself in them.

The second Saturday in May was just another lovely sunny day in North Carolina, however it was the day of the Big

Bake and Craft Sale as well as the Farm Market Day, and that was how we advertised it in the newspapers near and far. Lots of people apparently read the ad and thought "what a lovely day for a ride in the country", and found their way to our farm gate. We were swamped. Thank goodness the hens had cleared the edges of the drive on both sides so people could park there. The buses from the senior residences were busy bringing loads of people with their paintings, baskets, embroidered items, pocketbooks, birdhouses, lawn ornaments and whirligigs. The tables from the church were used. The ladies quilting club brought a beautiful double bed quilt in the "Dresden Plate" pattern. Brian put the quilt up on display and suggested tickets be sold on it and the draw could take place later, if the ladies approved. They were tickled pink that their quilt could generate quite a bit of money. Mertie rushed off to get another pickle jar, while one of the Ag girls ran off tickets on the computer with a number on each end and the name address and phone number on the stub. I made up a sign and Mrs. Meriwether sold the tickets—"I might be in a wheelchair, but I can help". We set her up at a card table in front of the quilt.

The twins were out in their carriage so I could push them around to the screened porch at feeding time. They were sleeping longer now and all night.

Car after car pulled in and Brian guided them to a parking spot up and down the driveway and around the barnyard turnaround. A huge crowd formed early, and even though it was changing continually, there was a crowd all day long. We were so thankful we had installed that bathroom off the dairy plus we had rented four "Johnny Pots", too.

The seniors, tired and happy after their day in the sun, climbed on the buses for a well deserved nap before supper. The quilting club asked us to take charge of the quilt. Brian assured them he would make a proper frame and it could be hung at church and any other fund-raisers. We would keep them posted on the amount raised, as time went by.

Our Ag girls had been wonderful, helping with the seniors, and carrying purchases to people's vehicles. They didn't want to take their pay for the day, but we insisted and they went home happy, tired and loaded down with their buys.

Patsy and Mick went home wanting to tell those at home how much had been raised for the "building fund," as it was now called.

The ladies from the church had completely sold out by noon and were as pleased as Punch.

As Alex and Elsbeth left, Elsbeth gave each of is a hug and remarked, "Ye are a talented boonch, I'll say that fer ye."

We retired to the kitchen. Mertie made tea with our new electric kettle, as I set out the egg sandwiches and potato salad Mertie and I had made the night before. We added homemade pickles. Dessert was ice cream ordered from and delivered by B&M Home Dairy. It was "Salty Butterscotch" flavor. We were tuckered out but satisfied.

"We'll display the quilt at the 'Chicken Dinner and Auction'."

"How are those plans coming along? I'm sorry I can't help more. I never dreamed I'd be so tired out. After all, they're only a couple of grapes."

Mertie laughed. "You have to take care not to get run down."

"That's what Doctor McCutcheon told me last week when he was here, plus your blood's a little low," Brian shared.

"Hah! That's why we are having spinach in everything, Mertie, and we had two batches of molasses cookies last week."

"Sweetheart, everything's coming along fine. Elsbeth is a crackerjack and she has inspired the ladies so there's no resentment at all, isn't that right, Mertie?"

"Oh, no resentment. She has the credentials and doesn't spare herself. She is a welcome addition to the group."

After church on Sunday, Alex announced a new total. We were still a long ways off, but greatly encouraged.

"Now I have some really good news. The Salem Presbyterian Women announced our problem at their Spring

Gathering. Donations are flowing in from every church in their catchment. On top of that, Mount Tabor Church sent us a variety of new goods for our auction—a couple of huge bags of dog food, a mesh playpen, a wicker plant stand, a doll carriage and a big wheelbarrow. This donated bounty was delivered by Leon and Ben Jacobs. I think you all know Ben and his sister Marty who worked for the MacKenzies when Brian was recuperating. The Jacobs family worked with Brian and Georgie to set up their organic farm over towards Cleveland. They have a farm market, too, so if you're over there or have family living in that area, please check them out and give them some business."

Besides sleeping all night, the twins were developing their own personalities.

"They sure change quickly, don't they, Mom?"

"They do and have you looked at their hair coming in at the back?"

We rolled them over a bit. "Oh, yes. Hey, Charlie's going to be reddy-blonde like you. Oh, look! Bess is going to have black hair like me and Dad." As Jamie and I squinted at their hair, Charlie suddenly grabbed Jamie's little finger while looking right at Jamie. Just then Brian came in the room.

"Look, Dad. Charlie's got my finger and boy! Is he ever strong."

We watched while Charlie smiled a bubbly smile and released the finger. "Good for you, Charlie. We're going to have so much fun."

Bess turned her dark eyes to Jamie. "Oh, you too, Bess." She solemnly stared at him. "I'm your big brother Jamie." Bess suddenly chuckled. Jamie was thrilled. "Will I be old when they start walking?"

"No, you'll be seven."

In June, for his birthday, Jamie got his first kilt, a velvet jacket, collarless shirt with a frou-frou of lace, good hard black shoes with buckles, white knee socks and a leather sporran. The kilt did up with leather straps and buckles and a two inch hem, so it would fit him for some time, even though he was tall for his age and growing like a weed. He was thrilled. "I'm just starting on the bagpipes, so now I can feel right."

# Chapter 43

One Sunday evening, Alex gave us a further update on the building fund. It was coming along fine, the dinner making just over two thousand, but still short.

"Alex, we could just give you a check for the rest. We have never touched the mayor's money."

"You haven't! You mean all that you have accomplished and the building you've done, wasn't from that money?"

"That's right. The mayor's money is invested, in case something catastrophic should happen to the community. We can get it if we have to, but we were determined to pay as we go, earning our money the same as everyone else. We wanted this farm to be a model of what you can do with what you have. When I got out of hospital, we sat down and listed what we had going for us, what was humanly possible, how were we going to get where we wanted. Two very shy people with no social graces. Georgie had the training, the dream and inspired me. She knew how to work with the government, and the agricultural college. Our customers became friends, and as they increased, we expanded our operation. We bought the smoker, and started making sausage. It was paid for in one month. Georgie plots every move, estimating the money needed and the results expected.

It's worked very well and we work together perfectly. Then Mertie came along and became instantly one of the team and more importantly, one of the family. The students we employ are encouraged, we teach them and they teach us, and we pay them well, and each goes back to school in the fall with a thousand dollar bonus as a thank you."

"So you see, Alex." I jumped in, "we could have just handed the money over, and that's what we planned to do if the money wasn't raised, but do you see how the participation has inspired us all. It's like giving a kid a bike—he won't value it. He'll throw it down without thinking. If he had to earn money to buy the bike, he would then appreciate, cherish and take care of that bike. This is the same. We all feel we have a stake in this fund raising. Our seniors have been a real inspiration to us all—once again the leaders they once were. Love it! Don't you?"

"Absolutely!"

"I was wondering if we could raise the remainder with a ceilidh, like Mertie suggested. We used to hold them in the little one-room schoolhouses, but perhaps we could hold this one in the high school auditorium, and as we are not at church, could we hold three 50/50 raffles?" I asked.

"What are those?"

"Sell tickets three for a dollar, and then draw one ticket, and that ticket-holder wins half of the take. By the time you sell the third and last draw, people are buying them by the arm's length and fifty percent is a worthwhile sum."

"How do you know about this, Georgie?" Brian asked curiously.

"Student events always have 50/50 draws. I understand the ones in the student pubs generate big money."

"Sounds good," Mertie exclaimed, "what do you think, Alex."

"I didn't hear a thing. Go ahead," and he put his hands over his ears.

"Good on ye," Elsbeth clapped him on the back. "I knew pastors sometimes haf tae turn a blind eye, but in this case deaf ears." We all laughed.

"Why did the ceilidhs die out?" Mertie asked. "We haven't had one in this area for ten years or more. They hold a big one at Grandfather Mountain, I believe."

"Well, Drummond MacLeod was our piper to pipe the people in and get the evening started. He set the whole thing up, musically speaking. When he died at ninety-two, there was no piper and no organizer."

Mertie and I never said a word. Jamie looked at me and I shook my head.

"Besides a piper," Brian started, "what musicians would we need?"

"A pianist would be the basic need; a fiddler would be great and we have one—Jim Scott; then a drummer—that's Liam McCartney who plays that Irish hand-held drum—the bodhran. I could master of ceremonies, if you want."

"If we advertise it far and wide like we do our ads, where could people stay?" I asked.

"Say! What an idea! You know the Flemmings—Rita and John—who come to church? Well, they are starting a campground on the edge of the Pisgah National Forest. This could be a boon for them. They have two hundred acres, mostly wooded, and only ten acres are set up at present, but they could have camping in the rough, plus they have trailer hookups, and they have shower and bathroom facilities. If this was a success, it would surely be a bonus to them. It could jumpstart their business."

"Make sure them come and talk to us sometime and Georgie will tell them how they can clear the wooded area and lower their tax base at the same time."

"I'll send them over,"

"Let's have another public meeting and chew this over collectively," I suggested. "Make sure the Flemmings are there, because if people come from Charlotte, Asheville or Greensboro areas, the Fairfax will never be enough room."

"Wud Missus Haggard nae play the piano?" Elsbeth wondered.

"I'm sure she would. I'll ask her to come to the meeting."

"I'll play the pipes," Brian said quietly. Mertie, Jamie and I applauded.

"Oh, Brian, that would be terrific. I remember you starting to play when you were eight, but I never knew you continued."

"Drummond MacLeod was my teacher. He wanted me to play in public but I was too shy, but with Georgie, Mertie and Jamie encouraging me, I've more confidence now."

"He's a great piper. Just puts the hair up on the back of your neck," I laughed.

"Just the best," breathed Mertie.

Sunday, after church, saw us all assembled again. It was agreed a ceilidh would be held. Alex had already gotten permission from the high school principal and his board, as long as we paid for a janitor to be on hand, and took out our own insurance policy for that night. We decided on the Saturday of the Labor Day weekend to get the campers. The Flemmings were excited because as yet they were unknown and their campers had been sparse. Mrs. Gordon belonged to a Scottish country dance group in Greensboro and she could have them there and they could demonstrate the steps for each new dance. The church ladies said they would man the kitchen and have light refreshment for sale. The 50/50 draw was explained and approved, as long as Alex didn't mind. He demonstrated the ear thing.

"You know this could grow into a yearly thing. We could call it the Aberfoyle Springs Annual Fling," suggested Douglas Ferguson. "smaller, later version of the Grandfather Mountain Highland events."

Miss Bain, our secretary, said she would run a nursery if she could have one classroom that had a bathroom and was close to the auditorium.

The meeting adjourned with everyone optimistic. Now if only the weather would co-operate. We are subject to torrential downpours in late August and September, and while it wouldn't bother the dancers, it could deter the campers.

Plans were put in motion. Ads were sent. B&M Home Dairy and MacKenzie's Farm Market had huge posters. The menu of snacks was decided.

The Flemmings came over one morning early in the next week, and we told them how to make a contract with the government over the harvesting and planting of trees on their property.

"And can you cut firewood, because we need it for our campers?"

"When you make a deal with a lumber company, make sure when they trim that they leave the limbs off to one side.

Then you just have to cut it up as it seasons and you'll have all the campfire wood and kindling you need. Other than providing bathroom facilities and a place to eat, that's all you have to do for the forestry students—they are transported, fed and paid by the reforestation plan that also provide the seedlings. You decide with them where you want the trees taken out and where the new trees should go," Brian advised.

"I'll cruise your woods for nothing, just lunches. It will take a few days. Are you knowledgeable about identifying the various trees?" They said they weren't. "Brian will come with me and help with the inventory. We'll bring Jamie so we can teach him, if Mertie can mind the twins?" She nodded enthusiastically. "I'll give you a signed document that the government will acknowledge as I have papers that say I can do this work. We'll divide the work up so we are not there every day and we can stay ahead of our own work load, but over the course of the winter, we will get it done. The government charges quite a bit for this service so you can forget that cost."

They seemed absolutely overwhelmed and most thankful that we would see them through this transaction with the government.

# Chapter 44

In the Art Room, just off the auditorium, Miss Bain and her two assistants, Judy McDuff who was in a wheelchair but always ready to help, and Ruthie Balfour who planned to be a nurse in a few years, had set up "Baby Headquarters" as the sign read. There were changing tables, space for babies in carriers and two playpens for little toddlers. Any child older than a toddler was expected to join their parents and take part in the dancing. They would be swept up by a man, woman, teenager or even a small child like themselves. All were encouraged to dance every dance.

I went to check that the twins were still sleeping.

"Oh, your twins are adorable, Georgie. So sweet! Are they quiet? Both you and Brian were extremely quiet. You were very smart and yet so shy. I heard you were more active and merry at home. Are you happy, my girl?"

"Oh, so happy! Things have worked out well."

"Especially for Brian. I taught him too, you know. He was in my first class. I loved him. He was so full of despair and so very shy, he could hardly speak. I once said to him 'you know the answers. Why don't you ever put up your hand?'

'Oh, no, miss,' he said, 'they would think I was showing off.' The other children treated him badly. I kept hoping he would stand up for himself. One good smack would have sent them all a message."

"He doesn't have a temper or a mean bone in his body."

I went back to where we were all sitting. I could see Alex, Elsbeth and Mertie all sitting with their arms folded across their chests and a scowl on each face. What was the matter? As I came around a knot of people at the edge of the dance floor, I could see Brian, arms crossed and head down. Beside him, Jamie mirrored his father. Then I saw, sitting in my chair, with her back to me, a large woman with untidy bleached blonde hair like straw.

"Hello, Sherree Thompson!' I recognized the hair.

"Well, well, Georgie. I was just telling Brian what an old sober sides you were in high school." Her over-generous mouth was smeared with red lipstick, and her eyes were black caves. Across from her, Brian now looked at her stone-faced. "Always trying to better your marks. I can hardly believe you snagged Brian. He had some really classy ladies that would have liked to have a shot at him. He's a hottie!"

The music was just tuning up for the last dance.

"Shall we dance, Brian?" I asked.

"Oh, he doesn't want to dance. He just told me so."

Brian stood up, "Oh, I want to dance. With my wife!"

"Well, bye then. It was good to see you again."

Brian stopped dead in his tracks and turned back to Sherree. "What do you mean—AGAIN? I've never seen you or spoken to you before, but I sure know who you are and what you are. There's no 'again' about it."

He turned to me. His dark eyes were almost black and were snapping with inner fire. His jaw was clenched and his body was rigid.

"Brian! Brian! It's a waltz. Shall we show them how we can waltz?"

He looked into my eyes,then smiled and took me in his arms and we were off. Twirling, swooping, gliding across the floor. Brian's kilt swirling around his legs. My plaidie (tartan scarf) swung out behind me as the salmon-pink petticoat winked onto view. At first, we didn't realize the other dancers were melting away, until a spotlight came on us and we could see we were alone on the dance floor.

Up, down, and all around we went, responding to the music.

When the music ended, I curtsied to Brian and he gave me a bow, then he opened his arms wide and I flew into them and he swung me around. He put me down and we held hands as we bowed to each side of the room. The applause was thunderous.

Faces scarlet, we went back to our party where we were hugged by all. I noticed Sherree was nowhere to be seen.

"I guess I have to end these proceeding. Get the bagpipes ready, Brian."

Alex thanked everybody for their support and hoped they had enjoyed their evening "perhaps the first of many". That brought applause, foot stomping and vigorous noises that may have been rebel yells or perhaps highland howls. Alex gave a prayer for safe journeys home and finished with a Gaelic blessing.

Brian started up the pipes. Jamie in his "kit and caboodle" as Mertie called his kilt outfit, led off, followed by Brian playing "Will Ye No Come Back Again" leading the crowd out of the auditorium.

Mertie and I got the twins, thanked Miss Bain and her helpers and went home in the SUV. Brian and Jamie would follow in the truck.

# Chapter 45

Later in bed, I told him what Miss Bain had told me about him, "I told her you didn't have a temper or a mean bone in your body. That was before I saw how angry you were with that stupid Sherree Thompson."

"You know what went through my head when she said 'again'?"

"No, what?"

"Maybe I should have had a medical examination to prove I was a virgin. It's not just young woman that can have their reputations shredded by idle words. With that one word that woman could plant a doubt."

"Not in my mind. She was carrying on with the football team in the back of the bus coming home from away games when I still had my hair in braids. Did you see the looks she was getting from Alex, Elsbeth and Mertie? Even our son managed to look disgusted."

Brian started to laugh, "Could a man ever have better chaperones?"

"Brian, do you remember our wedding night? We were quite a pair of bumblers. First, you hit the end of my little nose with the end of your beak, causing me to wince and my eyes to water. It felt like my nose was broken.

Then your thigh or leg was across my groin. I could endure the pain for about thirty seconds, then, my leg went numb. It was like I was paralyzed."

"Then I flopped my full upper body weight on you and knocked the wind out of you. You were gasping like a goldfish out of water."

"But then we realized our noses had to be parallel, but facing in opposite directions, and then we sorted out the legs."

"And I learned to ease my upper body onto my forearms. Then things worked out. But you are right—what a pair of bumblers."

"Have you ever laughed so much in all your life?"

"I've never stopped laughing since I turned the knob on the church hall door and there you were."

"I think our sense of humor is what got us over the shyness. I think we have a healthy sex life, don't you?"

"Absolutely. We didn't need any papers to show we didn't know . . . ."

"How to sail in uncharted waters?"

"That too."

After a pause, I asked, "Did you ever think two shy people like you and I would ever waltz in front of a room full of people, all on our own?"

"No, and when the spotlight came on, and I realized we were alone, I faltered, but then I looked into your eyes and said to myself "My Georgie and I can do this.""

"I saw you tense and then relax and I just sort of melted into you and we danced like one person."

# Chapter 46

We had told Mertie and Jamie to sleep in and we would eat breakfast after milking. We got up at five thirty. Brian went to the barn and I went to the twins who were just starting to fuss.

Fed and bathed, they were in their playpen in the kitchen in front of the china cabinet. They were so adorable. If one reached for a soft toy at the same time as the other, the first one would pick it up and give it to the other. They were never competitive, but loving with each other. Both were very quiet, with their little heads close together "gobbelty-gooking" in their own lingo. We loved them so much, but Jamie adored them. He talked to them, sang to them, played the bagpipes for them, showed them his artwork and introduced them to Buster.

The television on the counter was on a regional channel. Brian and I, as usual, were side by side on the periwinkle pew. Mertie sat at one end of the table and Jamie sat at the other end. We were all silently, tiredly, munching away when Jamie shouted, "Hey. It's you guys."

And there we "guys" were, waltzing away on the television. "A fundraiser was held for the old Presbyterian Church in Aberfoyle Springs last night." The announcer was saying. "This video of the piper and his missus has gone viral."

We were dumbfounded. Later, we were applauded at church. Around three o'clock, Alex called to tell us they couldn't come for supper as both he and Elsbeth were busy taking calls on the telephone. People were calling to pledge money to the building fund, and promising to put the check in the mail immediately. Some were old friends who had moved away—like Mom and Dad, some were back sliders eager to assist, some were Presbyterians who lived elsewhere, and some were highlander descendants glad to see our community was keeping the old traditions alive.

On Monday afternoon at five o'clock, we were having tea before milking and the supper preparations swung into high gear. The television was on. We were watching CNN, a major national news channel, as was our wont at that time of day.

"Look at this" the lady announcer was saying. "This went viral to-day. It was a fundraiser for an old church in Aberfoyle Springs in North Carolina, on Saturday night. This is the piper and his wife. Have you ever seen a more beautiful sight? I've never seen a man dance in a kilt before, especially such a large man, but see how light he is on his feet. Look how slim she is with her red-gold hair. She just gave birth to twins five months ago. And this is their little boy." Jamie had his fists under his chin, his mouth in an 'O' and his face shining with pride.

Tears were flowing down my cheeks. "Brian, this is going all over the world."

He put his wet cheek on mine and held me close. "Buck up, mo chridhe."

"Don't you love to see Americans celebrating their heritage?" the male announcer was saying., "And do you know," Wolf continued, "a few years ago Governor Jim Hunt said there are more descendants of Scottish Highlanders in North Carolina than any other state, or country in the world, including Scotland."